I0690607

3 EROTIC GAY NOVELLAS

First Edition

Published by The Nazca Plains Corporation
Las Vegas, Nevada
2011

ISBN: 978-1-61098-099-9
Ebook:978-1-61098-100-2

Published by

The Nazca Plains Corporation ®
4640 Paradise Rd, Suite 141
Las Vegas NV 89109-8000

© 2011 by The Nazca Plains Corporation. All rights reserved.
No part of this work may be reproduced or utilized in any form or by any means, electronic or mechanical, including photocopying, microfilm, and recording, or by any information storage and retrieval system, without permission in writing from the publisher. Printed in the United States of America.

PUBLISHER'S NOTE

3 Erotic Gay Novellas is a work of fiction created wholly by *Hank Brooks's* imagination. All characters are fictional and any resemblance to any persons living or deceased is purely by accident. No portion of this book reflects any real person or events.

Male Cover Photo, Yuri Arcurs
Heart, Ba-mi
Art Director, Blake Stephens

DEDICATION

To all who celebrate diversity.

3 EROTIC GAY NOVELLAS

First Edition

Hank Brooks

CONTENTS

Contents continued...

THE TRANSPLANTED HEART

Chapter One

The small town of Arborville, a suburb of Atlanta, GA, has a population of approximately 7,500 pious, church going souls. There are three churches in town to choose from; Southern Baptist (all black), Southern Baptist (all white), and Southern Baptist (fairly well integrated.) Practically everyone in town goes to one of the three churches.

In the all black, and in the fairly well integrated churches, the good pastors always preached the lessons that Jesus has handed down to us, generally about the power of love and forgiveness. More importantly, they practiced what they preached.

On the other hand, in the all-white church, Pastor Jimmy Winningham kept up a weekly barrage of hate spewing sermons. In one way or another he admonished his flock to hate and reject every human being who wasn't white, Baptist and heterosexual. He swore that these folk were all bound to burn eternally in hell!!!

He was particularly venomous when it came to the 'queers.' He constantly blamed the homosexuals for every ill visited by God on this, His chosen planet. He reviled the 'gay agenda', which sought to convert our youth to their sinful ways. This was particularly ironic because not one member of his congregation would be inclined to admit that he had ever met a homosexual or heard of one living among them. The assumption must be made that in a town of 7,500 souls, at least a handful of gay men and women were unhappily buried in the closet, and would move out of town at the first opportunity. Poor Pastor Jimmy! He didn't have a clue, but he was one of those closeted homosexuals.

He would hurry home after church every Sunday and hole himself up in his small apartment behind the church. While his flock were all enjoying Sunday family lunches, Jimmy would whack off, all the while dreaming he was being raped by, or he was fucking, one of the handsome young bucks in his congregation. With all that going on in his masturbation fantasies, it never occurred to him that he might be gay, simply because he had never acted on his obsessions.

One Sunday morning, Pastor Jimmy pounded on his lectern, and advised his flock that all the 'queers' would most certainly populate hell. If nothing else, he was very repetitive, and in spite of his ranting, most of the congregation found their minds wandering away. His voice got angrier and angrier. His face became more and more pinched, and his eyes got beadier and beadier. He was only 38 but at the moment he looked 58, especially with his hair slicked back, giving him a wolf like appearance.

Suddenly, those who were not daydreaming noticed that Jimmy's neck had turned a deep scarlet. Slowly the redness was rising up his face. At last his forehead was blazing red, and then it turned ashen white as the preacher slumped to the floor.

The good people of Jimmy's congregation sent for the town's only doctor, who did not attend any of the three churches. He was glad to see that Jimmy was breathing on his own, but he had obviously suffered a massive heart attack. Clearly, you could blame the homos for Jimmy's heart attack, since he was raving against them when he collapsed. The doctor gave Jimmy interferon and forced an aspirin down him. He sent for an ambulance and Jimmy was transported to a very fine, well equipped hospital in Atlanta.

The doctors at the hospital performed a triple by-pass, but declared that the prognosis for Jimmy was not good. Unless he received a new heart within a month, he probably would not survive.

In a neatly kept white bungalow, about one mile from the hospital, dwelt eighteen-year-old Robbie Cutler. Robbie was out and proud, and had the support of his adoring parents. Unfortunately, Robbie was very effeminate, and very flamboyant. The not quite, but almost feminine clothes that he wore to school were scandalous. In school, he did everything he could to avoid attending PE, and finally the teachers allowed it, since nobody wanted him on their team anyhow. He was teased and abused constantly, but Robbie faced his tormentors, stuck out his chin and put on a 'fuck y'all' face.

About a week after Pastor Jimmy was admitted to the hospital, Robbie was walking home from school. He turned a corner, only to face his perpetual tormentors. One look at them and he knew that something had changed. Gone were the grins on their faces. They had always laughed and hurled epithets at Robbie, but had rarely actually touched him. Now they were not smiling and each of them held a baseball bat securely in his hands.

Robbie had never seen such hatred in their eyes before, but he had no time to think about it. He lost consciousness with the first blow of a bat. He never even heard one of them yell, "I'm sending you to hell, faggot." They beat Robbie repeatedly without mercy until the fun and joy left them, and they ran away.

Moments later a passerby spotted Robbie. He saw a bloody face and immediately called 911. By the time Robbie's parents reached the hospital, Robbie was on life support. His brain was dead and there was no chance of recovery. After several hours of grief therapy, the Cutlers agreed to pull the plug and donate Robbie's organs for transplant.

One of the doctors informed Robbie's parents that there was a rather young Baptist Minister in the hospital who would die if he didn't get a heart very quickly. If they were to request that Robbie's heart go to the minister, who didn't have much time left, he wouldn't have to wait his turn on the donee list. The doctors already knew that Robbie's heart would be compatible and receptive in Jimmy's body. The dear, kind Cutlers had never known a minister who was less than charitable and loving, and so they readily assigned Robbie's heart to Jimmy Winningham. They saw it as a sign from God and a good omen for Robbie.

When he woke up for the first time after surgery, Jimmy wasn't quite lucid, but he was aware of two things. First off, his chest pained him, but it was nothing he couldn't stand. It just wasn't that bad. Secondly, he no longer felt as if a vice was squeezing his body. For a few weeks prior to his heart attack, he had been feeling as if something was crushing him and now he felt nothing and he was free of the unknown grip and it felt good. Jimmy relaxed and fell asleep again. He slept until the next morning.

When he woke up, his eyes fixed upon a rather large black man. The man was smiling at him and he said, "Hi Pastor Winningham. My name is Peter. I'm your nurse this morning and I'm going to get you all cleaned up and fresh as a daisy in case you get some visitors today."

Jimmy thought back. In the days following his by-pass surgery, he had not had a single visitor. He had no reason to expect one now. Jimmy was a loner, and he liked it that way. Instead of ministering to his flock in their sicknesses or their mourning periods, he preferred to stay home alone and feed his hatreds. A strange feeling of guilt invaded his thoughts and he vowed to change all that when he got back to his ministry.

As Peter took a soapy sponge in his hand, and started towards Jimmy's brow, Jimmy started to recoil. No African skin had ever touched him before. Wisely, he came to his senses. He was in no position to complain to hospital authority. Peter bathed him all over and discreetly offered him the sponge and indicated that he should do his own private parts. The truth is that Peter was so gentle that Jimmy found himself totally enjoying his sponge bath. Jimmy was particularly impressed at the skill with which Peter changed his linen while he was still in the bed. As if he could read Jimmy's thoughts,

Peter said. "We'll get you out of bed in a couple of days and this will be a lot easier. When the stitches come out, we'll get you into a shower." That thought made Jimmy feel good all over. He liked Peter and the good work he did. He didn't think that he could ever show gratitude to a black man, but he did, and to his surprise, it didn't disturb him at all.

Peter was in and out of Jimmy's room all day. He had to administer more pills and more IV's than Jimmy could count. Each time he came in, he straightened Jimmy's bed sheets to make him more comfortable. At the end of his shift, Peter introduced Jimmy to the night nurse. Mandy was a young white girl just out of nursing school. She was as cute as a puppy, but Jimmy was to find out that she didn't have Peter's velvet touch. Jimmy was surprised that when Mandy left the room, Peter stayed behind and sat on a chair.

"I notice that you had no visitors today," Peter said. "Do you mind if I visit for a while?"

"Not at all, but don't you have family to go home to?" Jimmy asked.

"No sir," Peter answered respectfully. "I divorced about five years ago and my two boys are now in college. One goes to Tulane and the other goes to the University of Florida. My ex lives there now."

Jimmy was amazed. He never knew any black men who went to college. In fact, he knew very few white men who did. He was roused from his reveries when Peter asked him if he would like to meet the parents of the boy whose heart was now beating inside of him. "They want to meet you and wish you well, but I need to get your permission."

"Oh yes, by all means," Jimmy said and he meant it. He wanted to put his arms around these people and thank them for their singular act of charity. Jimmy was aware of his feelings, but frankly, he was confounded by them.

"Do you play cribbage?" Jimmy asked Peter.

"Yes, I love the game, but I don't have a board around."

"Could you bring a cribbage board tomorrow, and I'll challenge you to a game." Jimmy actually smiled at Peter and once again, he wondered what was going on with him. He decided he just felt good, and he should stop wondering why.

The next day Jimmy got two visits. The Cutlers arrived about 10 AM. The three of them embraced, cried, and tried to comfort each other. Things were going well until Jimmy asked a fatal question. "How did young Robbie die?" he asked.

Mrs. Cutler began to cry so Mr. Cutler said that Robbie was the victim of a heinous hate crime. "He was a loving person and a loving son, but none of that mattered to those bastards because he was gay. He never harmed a soul and he didn't deserve this at all."

Jimmy lay dumbfounded in his bed. The heart of a gay youngster was beating in his chest, sustaining him, keeping him alive. At first, Jimmy wanted to rip his heart out and die. Of course, he knew that thinking like that was irrational so instead he said, "Nobody deserves to die like that." Then he said to himself, *Thank you, Robbie, for your heart. I'll prove to you that I deserve it.* He began to cry so the Cutlers wished him well and left the room.

When they were gone, Peter came in with another round of medications. "Did you know that my heart donor was gay?" Jimmy asked Peter.

"Yes, everyone in the hospital was appalled at the brutality those animals inflicted on an innocent boy. As a minister, you'll have plenty of opportunity to speak out against such terrible hatred. I know you'll make Robbie proud."

Jimmy cringed and wanted to disappear from the room. "I'll do my best," he said.

"Do it for my boy in Florida also," Peter added.

"Your son is gay?" Jimmy asked. "But I thought he played football."

"Right! He's gay and he plays football. I hear there are lots of gay football players," Peter laughed.

Jimmy was too amazed to respond. He was getting quite an education in the big city.

"I've got the cribbage board," Peter said. "We'll have a go at it at the end of my shift.

"You're on."

Jimmy's next visitor arrived at about 2 PM. It was one of the hospital chaplains. Jimmy greeted him warmly even though he found out that Father Roger Graham was an Episcopal Priest. It was just nice to get visitors, especially another clergyman. They chatted for a while and Jimmy made him promise to visit again. Jimmy liked Roger. He was a little younger than he, but he was very handsome, and Jimmy felt himself wanting to be Roger's friend. In fact, Jimmy had a desire to masturbate for the first time since his heart attack. He was no stranger to whacking off, but he was surprised that Father Roger had that effect on him. He wondered if having a gay heart was making him gay. Strangely, he didn't care.

Just as Roger was about to leave the room another young man came in.

"Joey," Roger cried. "Where have you been? I haven't seen you in ages." The two men embraced warmly and then Roger turned to Jimmy.

"This is Rabbi Joseph Brill, Jimmy. He roams the hospital halls also, so I guess you'll see a lot of him before you go home." Jimmy had never seen a Jew in his life, much less a rabbi. Where were the horns, the hooked nose? The young man standing before him was good looking. His hair was stylishly cut and he didn't look any different from anyone Jimmy knew.

"How's your boyfriend?" Joe asked Roger.

"It's off again, on again," Roger answered. "Right now it's off. I guess I'll have to keep looking for Mr. Right."

When he left the room, Joe sat down in the chair next to Jimmy's bed. "It's nice to meet you at last," Joe said. "Your story is all over the hospital."

"What do you mean?" Jimmy asked.

"Well, it's all about the irony. A young boy is murdered in a hate crime and God directs his heart to a clergyman. It's the stuff O'Henry stories are made of."

"I suppose," Jimmy said. He had never heard of O'Henry. "Now I'm under pressure to be worthy of it."

Joe smiled and laid his hand on top of Jimmy's. This made Jimmy distinctly uncomfortable, but he said nothing and he didn't move.

To break the silence he asked, "Is Father Roger gay?"

"Oh yes. He never hides it. His entire congregation knows."

"Wow! Unbelievable. How about you Rabbi? Are you gay?'

Joe broke out laughing. "Hell no!" He reached into his wallet and pulled out a picture. "This is my wife and son," he said. Jimmy looked at the picture. Joe's wife had blond hair and blue eyes. She looked like she could have been a cheerleader for Bama. His little son was also blue eyed and had red hair and a freckled face.

Jimmy stupidly said. "Your wife's not Jewish, is she?"

Joe laughed again. "Sure she is. 100%. Look, the reason for my visit is to clue you in on a few things. The Cutlers are members of my congregation. When the story got around, dozens of my congregants came to the hospital and donated blood for you. They wanted to keep Robbie's heart alive through you. They don't expect any thanks, but it would be nice if you sent our temple a little note when you are up to it." He handed Jimmy his card with the temple's address on it.

After Joe left with a promise to visit again, Jimmy had time to think. His whole belief system was falling apart. The kindest, most intelligent nurse he had ever met in his life was black, and his son was gay, but he played football for the University of Florida. The hospital chaplain was also gay, and the rabbi and his family didn't look any different than the people who lived on his street. The Cutlers didn't look different either. Most amazing, the heart beating inside of him and keeping him alive was Jewish and gay, and it had been fortified by other Jewish blood. Jimmy's mind was working overtime trying to reconstruct his prejudices, and this was causing too much stress to his belief system. Fortunately, he was saved by the bell, when Peter came in to play cribbage.

The next morning after his sponge bath, Peter announced that he had orders to get him out of bed and walking a little bit. Jimmy's new heart was working well and showed no signs of rejection. Jimmy was convinced that Robbie was making sure of it. He was also sure that Robbie had not gone to hell, but was looking over him in heaven.

Peter walked him to the bathroom so that he could try to pee standing up and go potty in a normal position. Bed pans were so awkward. Jimmy was frightened but Peter left him alone. When he was finished, he washed himself and looked in the mirror. He could not believe what he saw. Except that he needed a haircut badly, he looked ten years younger. In fact, he looked younger than his 38 years. All the wrinkles, or rather stress marks, on his face were gone. His ashen complexion was a healthy, ruddy color. Overall there was a look of happiness and relaxation in his reflection. He thought, *Robbie, whatever it is you have done to me, I like it. Thank you.*

When he got out of the bathroom, Peter was there to make sure he was all right. "Can you get me a barber?" Jimmy asked.

"No need," a familiar voice said. "I brought my personal barber to take care of you. "Mark, make this man look like a million bucks," Roger ordered.

Well this is one stereotype which didn't shatter, Jimmy thought. *Bill is a hairdresser and as flaming as they come.* Jimmy was surprised that he was able to let Bill touch him, and that he didn't turn to stone or spontaneously combust.

When Mark held a mirror for Jimmy to see the results of his makeover, Jimmy almost cried. He never knew how handsome he was. A new do can't make you change from ugly to handsome, but a new attitude can. At the moment, Jimmy didn't hate anyone. He even loved himself, and the face staring back at him was radiating joy and love. *Thank you Robbie for your heart.*

Finally, everyone left the room and Roger and Jimmy were alone. Roger took Jimmy's hand in his and shivers ran up and down Jimmy's spine.

"You look fantastic," Roger said. "I just hope you feel as good as you look." As he said that, he squeezed Jimmy's hand. Jimmy held back tears.

"Forgive me," Jimmy said, "so that I can forgive myself."

"For what?" Roger asked. He was truly confused. He didn't know the old Jimmy.

"Until I came to this hospital, I never knew a single black man, or a Jew, or a gay person, but I raved and ranted against them. Robbie knew that we are all the same underneath. We are all God's children. Robbie's heart is now my heart and now I can see all that he saw. I will never betray Robbie's heart so please forgive me and ask God to forgive me."

Without realizing what he was doing, Roger wrapped Jimmy in his arms, and held his head close to his chest. "God and I have forgiven you. Now you must forgive yourself."

Jimmy looked up into Rogers dark blue eyes. They smiled at each other.

"I know it's crazy and probably immoral," Jimmy said, "but I love you, Father Roger."

"The feeling is mutual," Roger said as he leaned down to kiss Jimmy on the lips. Jimmy offered no resistance even when both their lips parted and he could taste Roger's tongue.

Chapter Two

Jimmy spent almost two months in the hospital, and the doctors told him he would need another two months of physical therapy and special cardio-vascular exercises before he could return to work.

Roger was there every day, unless his church duties called him away. He made sure to minister to Jimmy's emotional and spiritual needs. The two pastors created their own little prayer service and performed it every night before Roger went home.

Peter was there every day also. He ministered to Jimmy's physical needs and between Roger and Peter, Jimmy was flourishing. He grew stronger every day and every morning when he shaved, the face in the mirror seemed to grow younger and more handsome. The heart which beat within him was transforming the rest of his body and all of his soul. He had never been so happy, and he would start to cry tears of joy at odd times and unexpected moments.

When the time came for Jimmy to leave the hospital and begin physical therapy, Roger insisted that he stay with him until he could return home and live an independent life. Jimmy offered no resistance. His gay heart was so in love with Roger, he would have done anything to be with him.

When the doctor came to speak with him prior to his discharge, he bombarded Jimmy with instructions, diets, exercises etc.

"Any questions?" the doctor asked.

"Yes, doctor. How soon can I have sex?" The doctor broke out laughing.

"Any time you want to play, go right ahead. But just like anything else in life, perform in moderation and don't overdo. May I ask if you and Father Roger are finally going to do the deed?"

Jimmy turned beet red. He would have fled and hidden if he could have, but his brave new heart smiled at the doctor and he nodded his head. The doctor gave Jimmy a hug and admonished him to call anytime if he had a problem or needed answers to questions.

About an hour later, Roger came to take Jimmy home. All that was available for Jimmy to wear was what he was wearing when he was admitted to the hospital. The suit was now ill fitting. Jimmy was 25 pounds lighter. "I think I've got stuff at home that will fit you," Roger said. "If not we'll go on a shopping spree."

The two men were very nervous. They realized that when Jimmy walked into Roger's apartment their lives would be different forever. They were looking forward to it, but nevertheless they were two nervous Nellies. They didn't speak to each other in the car at all until Roger pulled into his parking space.

Jimmy turned to Roger and said, "I love you, you know, with all my heart and soul. I know God brought us together and he approves. I am so sorry for how I used to curse gays." He started to cry.

"Hush, love," Roger said. "That's all in the past. Let's look to the future and plan for it."

"I'm scared. I want to make love to you, but I don't know how."

"We'll have so much fun while I teach you," Roger laughed. They entered the apartment building Roger lived in. In the lobby and on the elevator, they encountered several people and everyone said hello to Father Graham using his name. Jimmy knew that none of his flock ever greeted him, and these were just neighbors, not congregants. It seemed that everyone loved Roger and the heart inside of Jimmy was pleased.

Roger had a one-bedroom apartment with a queen size bed. Jimmy had slept alone all of his life and he wondered how he would manage. The rest of the apartment consisted of an eat-in kitchen and a living room. There was only one bathroom. Laundry facilities were down the hall.

The walk across the parking lot had tired Jimmy so Roger sat him down on a reclining chair in the living room. He took Jimmy's suit jacket and hung it in the bedroom closet, which had plenty of room.

"Just relax," he told Jimmy. He took a big plastic bag that the hospital had given him and emptied the contents on the kitchen table. There were at least a dozen pill bottles on the table. Roger read the labels, and placed the bottles in neat piles on the pass through ledge between the living room and the kitchen. They were sorted by the time of day each pill was to be taken. Then he took a batch of prescriptions from his billfold and put them in the cabinet above the pills. When he was done he took a glass and placed four pills in it. Then he filled another glass with water and brought both glasses to Jimmy, who was looking at Roger and smiling.

"You're due for these now," Roger told Jimmy. Jimmy swallowed the pills, drank all the water, and handed the glasses to Roger.

"I'm so sorry to be such a bother," Jimmy apologized.

"This is how much of a bother you are," Roger said. He leaned down and kissed Jimmy rather sensuously on the lips.

"Wow!" was about all Jimmy could say.

"Are you comfortable there baby or would you like to go to bed?"

Jimmy was still nervous about the sleeping arrangements and wanted to delay things so he said he was just fine. "This way I can watch you doing your household chores," Jimmy joked.

Late in the afternoon, the doorbell rang and Roger went to answer. There stood Peter with a bunch of roses. "I'll bet you thought you were through with me," he said, and he ran over to Jimmy and the two men embraced.

"In fact, you'll see a lot of me. After spending so many hours chatting with Father Roger, I decided to attend his church. I'm a regular now and I'm not going anywhere. Rog introduced me to his secretary, Ellie, and she knocked me out. We've been dating for a while now."

"Why you old coot," Jimmy said. "Good for you." Jimmy wondered if Roger's secretary was white or black and was about to ask when he suddenly realized that he didn't give a damn. That issue was between Peter, Ellie and God, and none of his damn business. When Jimmy realized that he didn't care, you could have knocked him over with a feather.

"Stay for dinner?" Roger asked Peter.

"No thanks. Ellie and I are going to see the new James Bond movie tonight, but I'll take a rain check."

"Before you go Peter, there's something I want to show you and Jimmy." He went to a bookcase and retrieved a picture album. "About six months ago several of our local churches had an interfaith service at Joey's temple, and I took some pictures. I believe Robbie Cutler is in one of them."

Once again, Jimmy was flabbergasted. He could not conceive of an interfaith anything. Roger flipped the pages until he found a picture of the Temple Choir taken during the service. He showed the picture to Peter and Jimmy. "There," he pointed, "in the back row." There was a visible gasp from both men. The face looking back at them could have been Jimmy's younger brother. Before his heart attack, Jimmy could say that he looked nothing like Robbie, but he knew that he had been transformed in body and soul and now the resemblance was uncanny.

"He was a good looking kid," Peter said, and Jimmy started to cry.

"Life is so unfair," he sobbed.

"Please don't say that," Roger said. "Robbie died a martyr so that you could live, and so that we could be together. There's a reason for everything."

"If I ever preached that," Jimmy answered, "I didn't believe it until now."

After Peter left, Roger made a simple dinner, a salad of greens and tomato, chicken broth served with Ritz crackers, and black coffee. After dinner, they watched TV for a while, and then Roger suggested they turn in. Jimmy's heart skipped a beat in anticipation, but he still tried to delay.

"I need to make one phone call to the President of my church board. I have to find out if I still have a job. Nobody has attempted to contact me and I haven't attempted to contact them either."

Jimmy took out his cell phone and found Dan Sommers in his speed dial. Some part of him hoped Dan wasn't home, but he really wanted to get it over with. Dan answered after the second ring.

"Dan," Jimmy said cheerily, "It's Pastor Winningham. I'm finally well enough to call you. I had a heart transplant and as you can imagine it's a slow recovery process. I was released from the hospital today and need another two months of physical therapy before I can return to work."

There was silence for a while and then Dan answered. "Gee, Jim, we hadn't heard if you were alive or dead so we hired us a young man just out of seminary. He's from Florida and has been with us for two weeks already. I am so sorry, man." Dan expected to hear a few expletives, but what he heard shocked him.

"It's really all right Dan. It's about what I expected. I was never popular there anyway. I've changed a lot. Could I ask one favor of you, please?"

Please! Dan couldn't believe that Jim had actually said, *please.*

"Sure, I'll do what I can."

"As soon as I'm able, I'll be coming home to pack up my clothes and stuff. When I do, will you let me say a few words to the congregation? It will be short and sweet, I promise. I really need to apologize to them and undo some of the injustices I committed."

Dan had no idea what Jim was talking about, but he felt that the congregation owed Jim that much. After all, they had pulled the rug out from under him so to speak.

"Of course, Jim. Just let us know when."

"Thanks Dan. I'll be in touch." He hung up and looked wistfully at Roger.

"Well, I kind of suspected it, but I am currently unemployed."

"I heard what you said about one last word to your old flock. I've got a vacation coming up. We can go get your stuff then and you can preach your last sermon at that church. I sure hope it won't be your last sermon anywhere."

"Yes, we'll talk about it, but it won't be a sermon, just a little speech. I'm tired now and I think I'd like to go to bed." Jimmy winked at Roger as he said that and Roger smiled back.

Jimmy's heart was beating so fast, he thought that he might reject it, but Roger put his arms around him and slowly he calmed down. He returned Roger's hugs and felt Roger starting to undress him. He helped Roger along and then he started to undress Roger. They hung their clothes neatly in the closet. They put their socks, shirts and underwear in the hamper and for the first time faced each other naked.

Jimmy was scared and flaccid, but Roger was hard. Jimmy took note. Roger was about six and a half inches erect and uncut. Jimmy knew that he was about seven inches hard, and he was circumcised. He was shaking like a leaf. Once again, Roger embraced him and calmed him down. Jimmy could feel Roger's hard member against his thigh and he began to erect. Roger smiled and kissed him gently on his lips.

"Come with me," Roger instructed, and he led Jimmy into the bathroom. He turned on the taps in the shower and waited to enter until the temperature was adjusted to his liking. He entered the shower and Jimmy was about to follow when he stopped.

"Roger," he said, "I have a confession to make. I'm a virgin."

"I know that," Roger said and I promise to be gentle and go slow."

"No, I mean I'm really a virgin."

"You mean you have never been with a woman either? My God, you're pushing forty."

"I know. It just never happened for me before. Maybe I've been gay all my life and never knew it. I just wanted you to know how happy you make me. I truly love you."

Roger grabbed Jimmy in a bone crushing embrace and walked him into the shower. "Let me do all the work," he said to Jimmy. "Just follow my lead." Roger took the bar of soap and proceeded to soap Jimmy wherever he could. He didn't hold back. He washed every opening in Jimmy's body except his mouth. When he inserted his finger into Jimmy's ass hole, the poor man almost fainted and cried out in joy.

"Tonight," Roger said, "we are going to mutually masturbate each other, and that's it. We have a lifetime to explore our bodies and give each other the ultimate of all pleasures, but for now I want to go slow." He then turned Jimmy around so that his back nested against Roger's chest. Jimmy could feel Roger's hot, hard cock probing against his ass hole, but Roger made no attempt to enter. Jimmy wasn't sure if he was disappointed or relieved.

Roger soaped his palm and reached around Jimmy. He wrapped his fist around Jimmy's cock and slowly and rhythmically began to stroke.

"Roger honey, that feels so good. I don't think I'll last long. It's been weeks since I whacked off."

"Let yourself go, sweetheart. Don't hold back."

Jimmy didn't hold back. Seconds later he was spurting all over the shower wall, and gasping for breath. Roger became concerned.

"Are you all right?" he asked.

"Never better sweetheart. It's just that it's been so long." Jimmy turned around and began to kiss Roger with deep passion. Then he grabbed Roger's cock and started to stroke it. He had never held another man's penis in his hand before. If he ever thought it would disgust him, he was very mistaken. He got so lost in how good it felt, he almost missed the signs that Roger had cum. They were facing each other and Roger's cum was spurting all over Jimmy's chest and belly. They remained that way a long time, kissing each other and fondling until they were beginning to look like prunes.

They slept naked, of course, and fell asleep holding onto each other's rods.

In the morning, Saturday morning, Roger gave Jimmy some casual clothing to wear. He served juice, coffee and toast for breakfast, and made sure that Jimmy took his morning pills. Jimmy was very silent so Roger was prompted to ask, "Are you all right this morning after having gay sex last night?"

"Yes, teacher. Let me assure you, I'm just fine. I can't wait for your next lesson. After what we did last night, I still feel like I'm a technical virgin."

"Good! I was a little frightened that you would be grossed out," Roger said.

"No way! Let me assure you that Robbie's heart was elated."

Roger put his arms around Jimmy. "I have to visit three people at the hospital, and then I have to get to the church and fine tune my sermon for tomorrow. Will you be all right?"

"Don't worry, I'll be fine. I intend to spend the day on the recliner watching television. But tomorrow is different. I want to go to church with you."

"That will be wonderful darling. I'll be able to show you off to everyone. Just remember that your pills are all laid out. Don't forget to take them when due."

"I promise. Now you promise not to worry about me."

When Roger left, Jimmy dozed off on the recliner. He began to dream. In his dream Robbie came to visit him. Jimmy was a little annoyed at first because Robbie was wearing clothes that could be worn by a boy or a girl, but no real boy would wear that. Robbie smiled and the clothing issue was dead. The beautiful face smiling at him warmed him from head to toe. *I am so proud of you,* Robbie said. *You are consumed by love and it is a joy to look upon your face. You are so lucky that Roger loves you. Please be open to his needs, and I don't mean only physical. Fulfill his spiritual needs as well.*

"I will. I promise. I love him." Jimmy felt someone's lips on his. Robbie was kissing him. *God has blessed you,* the apparition said, and disappeared. Jimmy woke with a start. He remembered everything about the dream and concluded that it was no dream at all.

God has blessed you, the ghost had said. Jimmy's whole body warmed as he remembered those words. He remembered to thank God as he fell fast asleep again.

He was awakened by the ringing of the telephone. He picked up the receiver. He expected to hear Roger, but it was a parishioner looking for his pastor. Jimmy introduced himself as Roger's friend and was prompted to say, "Maybe I can help you, I'm a pastor too."

"I don't know," the man said. "I know that Pastor Roger is gay and I can speak freely with him."

Again something prompted Jimmy to say, "I'm gay also. Roger and I are friends."

"Wow, OK then, here goes. I'm 22 years old, pastor, and I have never given much thought to my sexuality. I figured that someday I'd meet the right girl, get married, have kids, all in that order. But so far I haven't met the right girl and I have never been with a woman. Do you think that's strange in this day and age?'

"Not at all, young man. You should never do anything that makes you feel uncomfortable. Age is not a factor."

The youth continued. "Recently I met a guy at a party. We hit it off real good and started hanging out together. I began to realize that it was always just the two of us. He never asked me if I would like to double date or anything, and I am content that it is just the two of us. Last night he came out to me. I was pretty shocked. He told me that he had feelings for me and he wanted me to know because if I didn't feel likewise, it would be best to go our separate ways."

"How do you feel about it? Would you like to pursue it further or are you sure you are straight and want to squelch it."

"That's my dilemma. I always thought of myself as straight, but ever since I met this guy, I fantasize about him when I am whacking off. Oh, excuse me pastor."

Jimmy laughed. "No need to excuse yourself. Pastors whack off too."

"I suppose," the young man said glumly. "So how do I find out?

"Well," Jimmy said, "it's not uncommon for a gay man to experiment with a woman or a straight man to experiment with a gay man. You'll either love it or get grossed out, but at least you'll know. If you like this guy, don't give up on his friendship even if sex is out of the question for you. Continue to hang out with him and see how it goes. When you are ready, if you ever are, have sex with him and find out where your heart is, but don't push anything. Let whatever happens, happen." As he said that, his own gay heart skipped a beat.

"Would God condone my sleeping with a man if I turn out to be straight?" the young man asked Jimmy.

"God loves you and I am sure he loves your friend. That's all that matters. I hope I have helped."

"Yes Pastor, yes you have."

"Please let Roger and me know the outcome."

Chapter Three

After the young man hung up, Jimmy had second thoughts about how effective he had been. He was kicking himself for telling the man it was OK to experiment with gay sex. Then he rationalized that he had also said not to push it, and to experiment only if it felt right. Well, what's done cannot be undone. In fact, he felt rather good. He had just done some ministering and that was what he was trained to do. He decided to surprise Roger and have dinner ready when he came home.

He opened the freezer and found some chicken breasts. In a basket on the kitchen table he found some baking potatoes. There were eggs in the fridge and bread crumbs and corn starch in the pantry. Jimmy defrosted the chicken in the microwave, and when the breasts were soft, he soaked them in the scrambled eggs, patted them on the starch and then the breadcrumbs. He found a cookie platter and put the breasts on the platter, which he then put in the oven to bake. His southern soul would have preferred to fry the breasts in corn oil, but he wanted to take good care of his new heart. On a separate shelf in the oven, he placed two potatoes to bake.

He was setting the table when Roger came in. "What are you doing? You should be resting," Roger said as he embraced Jimmy and kissed him hard on the lips.

"I slept most of the day, and I assure you, I'm up to this. You can finish setting the table, and put out any condiments you would like with the chicken and potatoes."

Roger changed into a pair of shorts and a sexy tank top shirt. When he came out of the bedroom, Jimmy distinctly heard Robbie say, *Wow!*

"Wow!" Jimmy repeated and Roger laughed.

Dinner was very tasty and Roger kept telling Jimmy over and over again how much he was enjoying it. During the meal, Jimmy told Roger about his dream.

"God has blessed both of us," was Roger's only comment.

Then he told Roger about the young man's telephone call.

"I hope he lets us know what happens. I wouldn't have told him anything different than you did," Roger said.

"I am so glad to hear that," Jimmy sighed in relief. "How is your sermon going?"

"It's finished."

"Can I hear it?"

"Yes, tomorrow in church. I wrote it for everyone, but it's really for you," Roger smiled at Jimmy.

"I'll just have to be patient then."

The day's events were not particularly strenuous, but they were a bit much for a transplanted heart. The moment the two lovers got into bed, Jimmy fell asleep just as he was hunkering up to Roger. Roger smiled to himself thinking that lesson number two would have to wait until tomorrow. His mind repeated Jimmy's words, "I'll just have to be patient then." As he thought that, Roger distinctly heard a young voice whisper in his ear, Don't *sweat it. You have a lifetime to love.* As he fell asleep his eyes were wet with tears.

When Jimmy entered St. Benedict Episcopal Church the next morning, he was awestruck by how ornate the décor was. His humble little Baptist church had no stained glass windows and certainly no statues of saints or of the Holy Family. Of course Robbie could read his thoughts, and he heard the boy whisper in his ear, *My temple has lots of stained glass windows, but no statues either.*

What's heaven like? Jimmy thought, hoping that Robbie could hear him.

Aah, I have no words.

Jimmy sat in the second row of pews. Roger had suggested that he sit in the first row, but he didn't want to be conspicuous. Peter and Ellie spotted him and sat down beside him. Peter introduced Ellie to Jimmy, and Jimmy hardly noticed that she was black. He was becoming color blind.

"It is so nice to meet you at last," Ellie said. "Father Roger never stops talking about you. You are as handsome as he said you were." Jimmy blushed a deep shade of crimson. He was totally unused to compliments.

Jimmy had never witnessed so much pomp and circumstances in his life. It seemed to him like a theatrical production by the time all the priests and deacons had finally walked down the center aisle and to the altar. He was awestruck by the swinging incense and the solemnity of the procession. Frankly he preferred the simplicity of his church, but he was not critical of what he was witnessing. It had a certain majesty.

Jimmy tried to follow the unfamiliar service, and at last Roger got up to deliver his sermon. For a moment, Jimmy could not breathe, but he heard Robbie telling him to relax and he did.

Roger smiled at his flock and welcomed them all to God's house on this beautiful Sunday morning. Jimmy realized that he had never welcomed his flock, but always dove right in to his fire and brimstone sermon. He wasn't regretful, but rather he was learning a new way.

"Our God be with you!" Roger intoned.

"And also with you!" the congregation responded.

"You know," Roger began in a conversational way, "the other day I started to list all the lessons I could think of that Jesus had taught us in his short three year ministry. My list included charity, forgiveness, love, service, loyalty to our fellow men, and loyalty to God. Then I tried to list these lessons in the order of their importance. That became a real challenge. Obviously they are all important.

"We are always influenced in matters of choice by what is going on in our lives at that particular moment, and I found myself returning over and over again to the lesson of love. Why? Because that is what is going on most strongly in my life right now." Roger smiled at his congregation.

The congregation all looked at each other and smiled right back at him.

Roger went on to describe all the different kinds of love; the love of parents and children, husband and wife, sister and brother, neighbors and friends. Then there was the hard kind of love; the almost impossible ability to love your enemy. "Jesus said that it was possible, and therefore it must be so." Roger paused here and smiled at his flock.

"There is a love, however, beyond all others," he said in deep and florid tones, "and that is the love of two soul mates. Sometimes two people fall so deeply in love on this earth plane, that their souls are destined to retain that love through all eternity. It might be the love of two friends, two brothers, a husband and wife. Who knows what fuses those two souls together? Imagine what a blessing it is from God, when two souls on earth find themselves so deeply in love that their love is destined to last until the end of time.

"My dear friends be happy for me. I have found my soul mate. I ask you to please join me in the social hall after the service so that I may introduce him to all of you." Roger then read a biblical verse apropos to his sermon.

"This is the good news," Roger concluded.

"Praise to you, Lord Jesus Christ," the congregation responded.

Roger directed everyone to his favorite hymn and the service concluded with everyone singing loudly and joyously.

In the social hall, Roger introduced Jimmy as Pastor Jim Winningham, and long before it was over, Jimmy's hand hurt from all the hand shaking and the well wishes. *If this had happened in my church,* he thought, *I would probably have been stoned.* A wave of remorse washed over him.

Several people invited the two pastors to lunch, but they declined. Roger explained that Jimmy was recuperating from major surgery and rest was essential. In fact, Roger hustled Jimmy back home as soon as possible. As soon as they got there, Jimmy stripped to his shorts and sat down on the living room recliner, and Roger made them salads for lunch. As he prepared the salads, Roger was quiet and Jimmy dozed off. As he slipped deeper into sleep, Jimmy distinctly heard Robbie. *There is nothing wrong with my heart. It will serve you for your entire life. You two need to get out more and enjoy the scenery.*

"Did you hear that?" Roger asked. His question fell on deaf ears. Jimmy was fast asleep. Roger looked at his sleeping partner. Jimmy's face looked so angelic that Roger nearly cried. *Yes Robbie,* he thought. *After lunch, I'm going to air him out in the park and take him out to dinner.*

If you had to create the perfect day, today would be it. Everything was perfect, the temperature, the humidity, the breezes, and the lack of clouds in the sky. Jimmy and Roger sat on a bench watching a girls' soft ball game. Somewhere during the game, Roger took hold of Jimmy's hand. They were in a public place and Jimmy wanted to pull his hand away, but his heart would not let him. Instead he smiled at Roger and said, "Robbie is definitely winning out."

"I love you," Roger whispered, "and we are going to celebrate tonight. I'm taking you to a very fine restaurant. We'll relax your diet a little for the occasion."

"I'd rather stay home and continue our lessons," Jimmy said.

"After dinner sweetheart! I won't neglect your education. I promise."

Roger had a filet mignon steak for dinner, and Jimmy splurged on a roast half chicken with the skin removed. He couldn't resist a little vanilla ice cream for dessert. He hadn't had ice cream in years.

"Thank you for dinner, Father," Jimmy said as they were driving home. "You sure know how to spoil a guy."

"You ain't seen nuthin' yet!" Roger joked.

They were standing in the shower. The water was cascading down their united bodies, as they soaped each other all over and allowed their fingers to enter forbidden erogenous zones. Jimmy was making little whimpering sounds. The joys of the flesh had been forbidden to him for almost four decades, and he could not believe how wonderful Roger made him feel.

His brain kept imploring God to forgive him for his transgression of having sex with a man, and for having sex as an unwed person, but his heart answered, *Nonsense! This is where you were meant to be. You are in the right place at the exact right time. You are with your soul mate. It is God's will.*

When they got into bed, Roger was afraid to place his full weight on Jimmy so he straddled him and supported his weight with his arms as if he was doing push-ups. It was uncomfortable but his thoughts were only with Jimmy and to please him. He leaned down and kissed Jimmy on his lips forcing them apart, so that their tongues could caress each other. Jimmy's whimpering sound resumed anew.

When Roger reached Jimmy's nipples and began to suckle them, the room was filled with Jimmy's cries of "Aah!" Roger continued downward, sucking Jimmy's navel, then his pubic area. At last, Roger began to run his tongue all up and down Jimmy's balls, which nearly caused Jimmy to pass out. When Jimmy felt the first stroke of Roger's tongue running up and down the shaft of his penis, he cried out, much to Roger's surprise, "Thank you God for this great gift!"

Encouraged by this outcry, Roger enveloped Jimmy's entire cock in his mouth and deep throated him. Jimmy wanted to cry out and warn Roger that he was about to cum, but of course, Roger knew that. When Jimmy came, spurting his jism down Roger's throat, he gave out one final wail and began to cry hysterically. He was still crying when Roger released him and lay chastely down beside him. "Now I know what love is," Jimmy cried to no one in particular.

"Yes, just as you said, it is one of God's many gifts to us," Roger affirmed his belief.

Jimmy said, "I can't now. I'm just too done out, but in the morning after we have rested, I want to do all that to you. I want to show you how much I love you."

"Yes, my darling, in the morning." They fell fast asleep in each other's arms, and as they did, they each felt a kiss on their cheeks.

"Goodnight Robbie," they said in unison.

Chapter Four

Roger arranged for a two week vacation shortly after the Easter Holiday, and Jimmy called Dan Sommers and told him that he didn't want to deliver a sermon, but he would appreciate it if he could say a few farewell words to the congregation. Dan was sure that it would be all right, but he gave him the new minister's telephone number so he could make sure that Jimmy was part of the service. "His name is Mark Sommers," Dan said. "He's my nephew actually."

There was a small one bedroom apartment attached to the rear of the church which had served as Jimmy's home for the five years he had ministered there. He wondered if Mark lived there now.

When he called Mark's number a sweet feminine voice answered. "Pastor Mark's residence."

"Is he at home?" Jimmy asked.

"Yes, may I ask who is calling?"

"This is Pastor Winningham."

"Oh yes. We've been expecting your call. It is so lovely to talk to you. Please hold. I'll get my husband right away. He's playing with our son in the back yard."

While he waited, Jimmy thought, *They have a back yard. It doesn't sound like they live behind the church.*

"Hello Jim," a friendly voice said. "I've heard so much about you. I'm delighted to be speaking to you." *If he heard so much about me why is he delighted to be speaking to me?* Jimmy wondered.

"It's nice to speak to you too, Mark. First let me ask you something. Is my apartment behind the church being used by anyone?"

"No, no, Jennifer and I have our own home. The apartment was too small for us and our son, and we have another one on the way."

"Wonderful, wonderful," Jimmy repeated. "Congratulations! Here's my plan. I'll come this Saturday evening and stay in my old apartment. I don't have many things, but I'd like to pack up what I need and take it back to Atlanta. I'm not going to deliver a sermon. It's going to be more of a farewell speech, so I think speaking after you will be appropriate, if that's all right with you."

"I like your plan," Mark said. "Is there anything I can do for you while you are here?"

"No, I'll be fine thank you, but I'll be bringing a guest, if you don't mind. He's a minister also and he has been my main caregiver all through my hospital stay and after my release. In fact, I am living with him right now."

"He sounds like a saint," Mark said. "I look forward to meeting both of you."

"Same here! God bless!" Jimmy signed off.

"He sounded very nice," Jimmy said to Roger. "I'll bet they all love him and were glad to see me go."

"I think that when you say goodbye to them, they might have a change of heart. From everything you have told me, you are not the same you."

"That's for sure," Jimmy agreed.

Jimmy found the key to his apartment under the welcome mat where he had always left it. He and Roger entered, and Jimmy turned on the light. It wasn't working.

"Oh great," Jimmy lamented.

"Is there a hotel we can go to?" Roger asked.

"Yes, about five miles from here. I always kept some candles and matches in a kitchen drawer. Let's see if they are still there before we go running off."

Sure enough, Jimmy found some candles. He lit one, and with its light, he retrieved a candle stick holder from a cabinet. With the aide of the lighted candle he led the way to the bedroom.

"Very romantic," Roger quipped. "It's a good thing that we are lovers or one of us would have to sleep on the floor." He turned his head toward the cot size bed.

"It'll be fun," Jimmy said, "but we won't be able to pack until dawn, and if we don't finish, we can continue after church. Just let's make sure to get out of here as soon as possible. I'm beginning to feel very apprehensive and uncomfortable."

"Yes, I promise. We'll get us out of here as soon as possible."

They woke early and packed Jimmy's meager belongings in the car. They were finished before the sun had fully risen. Then they went to a coffee shop to have a little breakfast.

Roger and Jimmy stood outside the small church as inconspicuously as they could. Jimmy was eyeing the crowd, looking for Dan Sommers. All the while, several people approached them, offered a handshake and welcomed the 'strangers' to their church. Nobody recognized the stylish, young Jimmy Winningham. Jimmy didn't realize that they didn't know who he was and he assumed that they had totally forgotten him in so short a time. He wanted to cry, but he heard Robbie laughing.

What's that about? He mentally asked Robbie.

No answer!

Jimmy was shocked to see a few black couples in the crowd. Then he spotted Dan and his wife walking from the parking lot. He started to walk toward them. He extended his hand and Dan looked at him quizzically.

"Hi Dan," Jimmy said. "It's so good to see you."

"Hi, young man, do I know you?"

Jimmy began to laugh heartily and with good humor. "Dan, it's me, Jim Winningham."

"Oh, my God! In a million years I would not have recognized you." Dan stared in amazement. "I know you had a heart transplant, but I didn't know it included plastic surgery."

"Not plastic surgery," Jimmy replied. "Just happiness, contentment, love, and an amazing care giver."

"You've met someone then. How wonderful!" Dan said.

"Miraculous," his wife said facetiously. Everyone ignored her.

"I'd like you to meet someone who has come to mean a great deal in my life," Jimmy told Dan and his wife. Taking hold of Roger's arm, he said. "This is Father Roger Graham. He's a chaplain at the hospital where I had surgery, and we have become intimate friends."

Mary Sommers looked at the handsome priest and her animosity disappeared. She took his hand to shake, and said, "It's so nice to meet you Father."

"Just call me Roger, please."

"I think it's time to go in now," Dan said.

Roger could not get over the simple service and wondered if it would even last an hour. He expected that Mark's sermon would be the better part of it.

Mark ascended to the pulpit, and smiled broadly at the congregation. He welcomed everyone to the little church and especially welcomed the visitors among them.

Once again, Jimmy wondered why he had never welcomed his flock. He guessed that it was like a given that they had to be there, so why waste the words?

Mark's sermon was short and sweet. It concerned charity, not only the money and the assets you give to worthy causes, but the charity you show to your fellow man. "That's the charity you give of yourselves to others. The more love and support you give to your fellow man, the more comes back to you."

When the congregation said 'amen' nobody said it more fervently than Jimmy.

At the conclusion of his sermon, Mark smiled at the congregation and said, "I have a wonderful surprise for you today. Our former pastor, Jim Winningham, has returned to us and would like to say a few words."

Jimmy distinctly heard a few groans and he also heard Robbie laughing. He hesitated for a few moments, and then rose and approached the pulpit. Instead of groans, there was a loud gasp from the assembled. They could not believe that the handsome young man approaching the dais was Jim Winningham. To add to the drama, Robbie walked beside him, and there appeared to be a light shining from Jimmy's body.

Jimmy had not confided in Roger, so Roger had no idea what his lover was going to say. He sat stiffly and expectantly in his seat.

"Thank you, thank you all," Jimmy began, "for welcoming me back." I promise to be brief. I know you all have your Sunday lunches waiting for you, and I have to return to Atlanta when the service is concluded.

"I just wanted to ask you all to forgive me." Jaws dropped all over the church. "I was a preacher to you, yes, but I was never a spiritual leader. For that I apologize. Recently I heard a sermon delivered by my good friend, Father Roger. This morning I heard another sermon by your wonderful pastor, Mark. Each in his way urged you to love and to be charitable. What a wonderful message, but hardly new.

"These are the lessons of Jesus, which these two fine young men have taken upon themselves to teach and to spread the good word to all who will listen. I distorted everything, every text that God gave us. I am aware that I preached hatred. I don't know what I was thinking. Again, I ask that you forgive me. I am truly changed. I have often heard the expression, 'born again.' If there is such a thing it happened to me.

"The new, healthy heart which beats inside of me was given to me, in an act of pure charity, by the parents of a teen age boy who was beaten to death. He was martyred for what he was, and Jesus surely wept at his death. That young man walks beside me, holds my hand, and guides me. I hear his voice and I know that he is my guardian angel. I promise you that I have learned love, charity and forgiveness, but I need you all to forgive me so that I can move on, and make my ministry meaningful."

Jimmy started to leave the pulpit, but to his surprise, Mark came to him and embraced him. When the congregation, including Mary Sommers, saw this they stood and cheered and yelled, "Yes! Yes! Yes!"

Jimmy was crying on Mark's shoulder as Roger took his hand and led him back to his seat. Mark chose a hymn of thanksgiving to close the service. Nobody sang louder or more joyously than Jimmy.

After the service he was surrounded by his former flock. Everyone wanted to shake his hand and wish him well. Others talked to Roger. They wanted to know about his church, and what magic he used to bring Jimmy to his senses. Roger just laughed and attributed the miracle to Robbie Cutler and Jesus Christ.

Mark could not get close to Jimmy so he approached Roger. "Please," he said, "it's not often I can sit and chat with fellow clergymen. Would you and Pastor Winningham come for lunch? Just give me an hour. There is so much I want to ask you."

"It would be an honor," Roger answered for both of them.

Jennifer Sommers served egg salad and chicken salad on a bed of lettuce. She provided biscuits with honey in true southern style. Everything was delicious. After lunch, Mark invited his two guests to sit with him on his veranda before they left. Jennifer served them iced tea and then left them alone.

Mark smiled at Jimmy and asked, "You said that your heart donor was martyred, Jim. How was he martyred?"

A tear came to Jimmy's eye. "He was gay and he was beaten to death. He was also Jewish, but there were a lot of Jews in his high school. He was often abused because of his sexual orientation, not his religion, so we are sure that was the reason for the attack. Members of Robbie's temple generously contributed blood to me to make sure Robbie's heart lived.

"But the real miracle came after the surgery." Jimmy continued. I met Roger and he began to minister to my spiritual needs. He visited me every day. His second in command was Robbie's Rabbi, Joe, and last but not least, a black, male nurse ministered to all my physical needs. From the start, Mark, I began to hear Robbie's voice. He assured me that his heart would last my lifetime, and it would be a long life. He told me that God had blessed me and to go out and preach love, not hate. He was gay and he was in heaven, not hell. What an eye opener. Speaking of eye openers, I looked in the mirror and saw that I had changed physically too. I was actually handsome and my face was full of peace. I hardly recognized myself. It seems most of your congregation didn't recognize me either."

Jimmy seemed to have finished his narrative, and Mark looked him straight in the eye and asked, "You two are a couple aren't you?'

Jimmy panicked, turned red and was speechless. Roger took his hand, and Robbie told him to calm down. "Yes, we are," Roger stated. "Given that Jim is a former homophobe, how did you know?"

Mark smiled. "My Uncle Dan has two brothers, my dad and one other, Paul. Paul is gay. He came out in high school, and he too faced daily abuse. Just imagine what it's like growing up gay in the Bible belt."

"I don't have to imagine," Roger said.

Mark went on. "Everyone in our family, my dad, Uncle Dan, and Jen and I, love Uncle Paul and his partner to death. If those two guys go to hell then I will stop believing in my faith. Somehow you two just reminded me of them."

Jimmy was cringing. He wanted to vomit. He thought back to all the times he had raved and ranted against gays, and Dan was sitting in his church all the time. How did that make Dan feel? Without realizing what he was doing, he began to sob and he yelled out. "Forgive me, please forgive me."

Roger and Mark jumped up and surrounded him with hugs.

"Not to sound like a Catholic Priest," Mark said, "but I'm pretty sure you were well forgiven in church this morning."

"Amen," Roger said.

When Roger and Jimmy went to their car to begin the ride home, Mark made them promise to stay in touch.

"And please let us know when the new baby arrives," Jimmy begged.

Chapter Five

Every day when Roger left to perform his pastoral duties, he believed that Jimmy was resting or going to physical therapy. A cab was always there to take him to and from his therapy, but he was not resting at all. Nothing could be further from the truth. Jimmy was searching the internet and making calls hoping to secure a position with a church in Atlanta. He wasn't too successful at first.

When asked about his availability, he answered, "In about six weeks." Then it was four and then two and finally he was given the go ahead by his cardiologist and he said that he could begin immediately. One of the churches that responded to his letter and résumé arranged an interview for him with the church board. It was for the position of assistant pastor. Jimmy didn't mind that at all. He just wanted to get back to work, and preach his new philosophy.

Jimmy immediately called Bill, the hair stylist, who came to the house and gave him a magical haircut. On the morning of the interview, he borrowed a suit from Roger's closet, and took a cab to the church. The cab stopped in front of the church and Jimmy got out. He stood gazing at the church and his heart skipped a beat. The church was almost as large as St. Benedict, and nearly as ornate, but compared to his old church it was practically a cathedral.

He stared at the name over the front door. CHURCH OF THE SAVIOR, and underneath that: A METROPOLITAN COMMUNITY CHURCH.

Jimmy had never heard of that church, but he had assumed that it was a Protestant church. He stood outside, hesitating to enter. He would not lie, but he didn't have to tell either, and he prayed nobody would ask about his sexual orientation. If they did, he vowed to tell the truth.

He heard Robbie giggling. *You'll be happy to tell them that you're gay.*

What do you mean? Jimmy thought.

No answer. Sometimes Robbie could be a big tease.

Jimmy had been told that when he entered the church, he should turn right and he would see a door that led to the church offices. Sure enough there it was. He knocked on the door and went in. There was an outer office for a receptionist, but the office was empty. In the rear there were two other doors and he could hear talking from behind one door. He approached that door and knocked.

The door opened, and a man in his early sixties was smiling at him.

"You must be James Winningham," he said extending his hand. "I'm Darryl Williams, Senior Pastor here. It's a real pleasure to meet you. Please let me introduce you. This is our Board President, Timothy O'Shea and another Board member, John Lafferty. We three will make the decision. We didn't want to overwhelm you with the whole Board of Directors."

Jimmy shook each of their hands and then sat in a chair that Darryl pointed to.

"Now Jimmy, I must tell you that we have already spoken to your references, the present pastor of your old church and the Board President. They both gave you high marks and explained why you left. How is your health now?" Darryl asked. Jimmy sensed that the question was asked out of concern and didn't seem to be part of the interview process.

"I'm great. My doctor has given me a clean bill of health. I can do anything I want within moderation."

"I'm really glad to hear that," Darryl said smiling. "I do have one concern. I know that you are a Baptist, but our service has a lot more ritual than you have. It leans towards Episcopalian. Do you think that you can handle that?"

Jimmy began to laugh. Then he said something so spontaneously, he wanted to die after he said it. "My lover is an Episcopal priest and I have been going to his church every Sunday for weeks now. I am very familiar with the service."

When he realized that he had just outed himself, he wanted to get up and run, so the reaction he got was amazing.

"I'm so glad you're partnered," Timothy said. "You surely must know that you are really hot, and having a partner will avoid distractions, if you know what I mean?"

Jimmy didn't know what he meant, nor could he fathom Timothy's reaction. He decided to remain silent, and not comment. He thought it would be best to see how this all played out.

Darryl continued. "After speaking to your references, we became convinced that you were the man for the job, but we would like for you to conduct the early service this Sunday, and deliver the homily before we make a final decision."

"How many services do you have on Sunday?" Jimmy asked in amazement.

"Two," Darryl answered.

Jimmy was thrilled, excited and scared, all at the same time, until he heard Robbie. *Relax Jimmy. This opportunity came to you through divine intervention. This church will become your home and one day you will be the senior pastor.*

"Let me offer some advice when you prepare your sermon," Darryl said. "Our church is all inclusive." Jimmy had no idea what Darryl meant. "Every Sunday our seats are filled with Christians of many religious backgrounds, but we also have non-Christians who make our church their home."

Jimmy couldn't remain silent any longer. "Why would non-Christians find a home in a Christian church?"

Darryl was amazed at the question. "Isn't it obvious to you that we are a safe haven? They worship here because they are in a place where being gay is OK. Jimmy, do you mind if I ask you how long you have been out?"

Jimmy started to laugh and cry simultaneously. He heard Robbie advising him to remain calm.

"Just a few short months," he answered. "I had no idea this was a gay church."

"Would you rather not serve here?" Darryl asked.

"Are you kidding? It will be a singular honor."

After the three men calmed him down, Jimmy said, "Let me tell you a story." He told them about Robbie Cutler, whose heart was beating inside of him. He even ventured to tell them that he could hear Robbie advising him. He didn't care if they thought he was crazy or not. "The heart that beats in my chest and keeps me alive, so that I can spread the word, is gay and Jewish. I believe that I fit the category of all inclusive."

The men were quiet when Jimmy finished. Finally Darryl said. "Can you be here Saturday afternoon and we'll go over the service together."

Jimmy could not wait for Roger to get home. He was too excited to prepare a meal, and decided he would take Roger out for dinner. He put on a pair of shorts and a muscle shirt. He sat in the recliner and waited. While he waited he thought about his sermon.

You'll knock them dead, Robbie said.

"What shall I talk about?" Jimmy asked.

It will come to you.

When Roger came home, he rushed to Jimmy and hugged him. Usually he found Jimmy preparing dinner, but when he saw him sitting on the recliner, he feared that something was wrong.

"Are you all right, sweetie?" Roger asked in concern.

Jimmy grabbed Roger's arm and pulled him forward so that he ended up sitting on Jimmy's lap.

"I've never been better," Jimmy said with a huge grin on his face. "I think I may have landed a job as assistant pastor at Church of the Savior."

"The gay church?" Roger asked utterly amazed.

"The very same. I preach my first sermon this Sunday morning."

"You rascal! How and when did all this happen?" Without waiting for an answer, Roger went on. "I'll take Sunday off and go hear you. I've been told that you're all fire and brimstone, and you send gays to hell." Roger started to laugh hysterically.

"You heard right, mister," Jimmy continued the joke. "Those queers are in for quite a surprise this Sunday." He too started to laugh and the only thing that stopped the laughter was that the lovers began to kiss.

"Now change into something sexy," Jimmy said. I'm taking you out to dinner at the gayest restaurant I know of, and I want all those queens to envy me."

"Envy is a deadly sin," Roger said.

"Then you and I will save their souls."

Of course Roger knew all about the gay church, and he was happy and comfortable to find that the service was almost like his service, but a little bit less formal. When he first saw Jimmy in clerical vestments, he was stunned. He thought that he was even more handsome than in shorts and a muscle shirt. He looked around the church and he thought, *it's OK to envy me now, you queens.*

For the past few days, he had bugged Jimmy to let him read his sermon, but Jimmy said what Roger had said, "You'll hear it in church." Roger had no choice but to be patient and extend Jimmy the same courtesy that Jimmy had extended him.

When Jimmy ascended to the pulpit to begin the homily, the men in the audience were drooling and the women were thinking what a handsome young man.

"Hi everyone. It's a thrill and an honor for me to be here with you this beautiful Sunday morning in this beautiful House of Worship." He had remembered to start by greeting the congregation. Then he continued.

"If I am really lucky, I'll be assuming my duties as your Assistant Pastor, so please don't fall asleep on me and please give me good grades, because I really want so much to be here for you." The congregation laughed. Encouraged by the smiles, he continued.

"You might have noticed that I came up here without any notes. It is my intention this morning to introduce myself to you. I want you to know who I am, where I came from, and my dreams and aspirations for you and the world at large. I really hope that after all that, you will want me to be your pastor.

"To begin with, I was ordained as a Baptist Minister. In a crazy effort to bury my sexual orientation, I became the most homophobic pastor this side of the Mason Dixon line, which made me pretty homophobic. Each Sunday I preached hatred from my pulpit, not only for gays, but for anyone who wasn't Baptist or white. Looking back on it, I was a pretty big boor. My message never varied. Then a few short months ago, I was literally reborn."

Jim went on to tell of his heart attack. He described Robbie's bashing and tears filled the church. "But in the end a miracle happened. I got Robbie Cutler's heart. I got a gay, Jewish heart, and I immediately began to change. I was overwhelmed with all kinds of strange emotions, strange to me, at least. Thanks to Robbie I learned to love the world and everyone in it. Robbie's heart beats within me; strong, healthy, loving, loyal and very much in love.

"One of the other miracles that Robbie gave me was the ability to face my own sexual needs and desires. One day the hospital chaplain came to visit me. When I saw him, I wanted to leap out of bed and make love to him. 'Smitten' is a very mild and understated word. I wish I could tell you how his beautiful face overwhelmed me and filled me with desire. I fell in love for the first time in my life at the age of 38.

Father Roger Graham is an Episcopal Priest. He serves at St Benedict Episcopal Church where he is the senior pastor. Because of him and his love, I have become a better minister. Because of him, I have an overwhelming need to serve my community, and whoever else might need me any place in the world. I often attribute the person I am today to Robbie and Roger, but I would be remiss if I didn't give credit to God.

"There are no accidents in the world. Is there anyone of you out there who can honestly not see how God maneuvered my life? He knew that I could be a better person, and he caused one event after another to bring me to this place, at this moment in time, exactly where he wants me to be. And I want to be here also, to minister to you and to serve you. I fervently pray that you will let me."

The congregation, thinking he was finished, began to applaud. When the applause died down, Jimmy said, "Before I leave the pulpit I want you to meet my partner and my soul mate." He motioned for Roger to stand up. More applause from the assembly.

Darryl approached the pulpit and embraced Jimmy in a bear hug. "Welcome to the church," he said. "Do you think you can repeat that little speech at the later service? I want everyone to meet our new pastor.

As happy as Jimmy had been since his heart transplant, this was the happiest moment of his life.

Welcome to your new home. He heard Robbie very clearly.

The second service was attended by twice the worshipers than attended the first service. Jimmy panicked a little bit, but he had Roger to calm him down, and he could feel Robbie's presence also. Between services he and Roger sat with Darryl in his office and sipped tea and scones. They were delicious and Roger asked where they came from.

"My partner is from England and he has mastered the art of scones. He'll be here for the second service and you'll meet," Darryl said. Then he turned to Jimmy. "I am really excited to have you join us, but I wonder if it won't hurt your relationship, if you two can't worship together every Sunday."

"We worship together every evening," Roger said.

"Yes, we have made up our own little bedtime prayer service so we will be fine. We both have our calling and we complement each other. We don't compete," Jimmy added.

"That's wonderful," Darryl said.

Jimmy's plea for acceptance was even better received at the second service than at the first. The applause was deafening. After the service, they joined the congregants in the social hall. Darryl was busy introducing Jimmy around and Roger was introduced to Darryl's partner. They began to chat.

"It's great to meet you," William said. "I grew up in the Anglican Church you know."

"Well, you are always welcome at my church anytime you want to come."

"I'm old and set in my ways. Thanks for the invitation, but I'll stick to my honey's church."

When they got home, the first thing that Jimmy did was to call Dan and Mark Sommers. He told them that the position was his and he thanked them for their recommendations.

That night as they were preparing for bed, Roger said, "We should do something special to celebrate your new position."

"What did you have in mind?"

"Well there is something I would love for us to do, but I don't know if you are ready and I hesitate to ask," Roger said.

"Don't be foolish. Ask! The worst that can happen is I'll say no."

Roger took a deep breath. "I'd like us to fuck each other," he said.

Jimmy broke out laughing and Roger got concerned. "I've wanted to do that forever, but you never talked about it, and I was afraid to ask you."

Roger smiled and grabbed Jimmy in a bear hug. "We'll go slowly," Roger said. It always hurts a bit when you start out, but in the end the pleasure is worth the little bit of pain. You fuck me first. No pain involved."

"No," Jimmy said. "That's a cop out. I want to get fucked first. You've done both, haven't you?" Roger nodded shyly. "Then you can teach me."

"Let's start in the shower," Roger said. They undressed quickly and when they were naked they fell into each other's arms. They began to kiss and fondle and neither wanted to move, but finally Roger said, "Let's go."

At first, they soaped and washed each other as they always did, but then Roger told Jimmy to turn to the shower wall and place his hands on the wall as if he was doing vertical pushups.

"Stick your butt out," Roger told Jimmy.

Roger soaped his hands until all he could see were suds. He placed his middle finger against Jimmy's crack and ran it up and down. All the while he kept advising Jimmy to relax. It took a while, but Roger could sense when Jimmy was thoroughly relaxed. He placed his index finger on Jimmy's opening. Jimmy tensed. Roger began to kiss the back of Jimmy's neck and urged him to relax. Slowly he started to insert his finger. Every few centimeters he stopped and asked Jimmy if he was all right. Jimmy would nod in between sighs.

When Roger reached Jimmy's sphincter he stopped. "This is it," he advised. It will hurt. If the pain is too much, please stop me. Once I get past the muscle, the pain will begin to go and the pleasure will be there."

"Go, honey. I want it real bad. Don't stop even if I tell you to." Slowly Roger proceeded. He felt the resistance of the virgin muscle but he kept going in ever so slowly. Suddenly he felt that he had gone beyond the muscle. His finger was sliding more easily and he was all the way in. He started to ream Jimmy's ass hole in an attempt to start stretching it. His finger touched Jimmy's prostate and Jimmy sighed.

"That feels wonderful. Don't stop," Jimmy said. That emboldened Roger to begin to insert another finger, his index. When he reached the muscle he asked Jimmy how he was doing and Jimmy could only mumble, "Don't stop" even though he was in pain. At last the second finger penetrated and now Jimmy's prostate was being massaged. All the pain was gone and Jimmy was in paradise.

"Please take your fingers out," he pleaded, "and give me the real thing.

Roger was happy to oblige. His cock met some resistance and some tensing from Jimmy, but finally Jimmy relaxed and Roger's cock slid right in. He remained still, and did not move for a moment and then he began to pump. They fucked in silence until Roger could bear it no longer. "How are you doing?" he asked.

"This is so wonderful. Why didn't we do this sooner? Can you try not to cum for a while?"

"Too late," Roger screamed, and he came gushing into Jimmy's ass. It took a few minutes for him to catch his breath.

"I almost came without you touching my cock," Jimmy told Roger.

"That's because my cock was massaging your prostate gland," Roger informed his lover.

"I need to cum badly," Jimmy said. "Can I fuck you now?"

"Yes, of course, but let's do it in bed with lubricant. I think you'll enjoy it more."

Jimmy did not bother to try to stretch Roger, but he went right in. Resistance was minimal. Jimmy had almost reached orgasm when Roger was fucking him, so he came swiftly. His orgasm was intense and his whole body bucked like an unbroken bronco.

Lying together afterward, Roger asked Jimmy which he liked better, oral or anal sex. "They are both wonderful," Jimmy answered. Your mouth is hot and wet, but so is your ass. The only difference is I feel more in control when I'm fucking you, like I might be able to control my orgasm and make it last longer."

"Yes, that's how I feel," Roger said. "Isn't it wonderful? We have a whole lifetime to enjoy it all."

As they were falling asleep, they distinctly heard Robbie. *It's about time you guys got around to fucking each other. What took you so long?*

Chapter Six

Jimmy assumed his duties the very next day, and within a month Darryl and William planned a much needed vacation. They were going to England for a month to visit William's family.

Roger and Jimmy fell into a happy routine. Every Sunday after church, they met at their favorite restaurant for lunch. It never failed that several of Jimmy's flock came over to say hello. The restaurant was in the heart of the gay section of town and was gay owned and operated. Never in his old life had any of Jimmy's congregation ever greeted him outside of the church. He delighted in these greetings and he could feel Robbie embracing him.

Jimmy was happy and content. Everything he had missed in his life was finally his; love, acceptance, friends, and a great sex life. Every night before going to bed, he and Roger recited a prayer that they had jointly written extolling God for the multitude of gifts He had given them. Every night Robbie joined them in prayer.

One Friday evening just as they were cleaning up after dinner, the phone rang. Jimmy answered.

"Father Roger, please," a familiar voice requested. Jimmy searched his memory bank, but could not place the voice.

"It's for you," he told Roger and handed him the phone.

"Hello," Roger said. "Can I help you?"

The voice on the other end of the phone identified himself only as Matthew. He said that he attended Roger's church, and Roger strained to remember him.

"I spoke to your friend, the other gay pastor, a few weeks ago, but I really need to talk to you, Roger. I'm so confused and I need your guidance."

"Of course," Roger said. "Can you meet me at the church tomorrow morning, say about 10 AM?"

"Yes, that will be wonderful. Thank you so much. I'll be there."

After he hung up, Roger said to Jimmy, "The young man said that his name is Matthew and he spoke to you a few weeks ago." The bell went off in Jimmy's head.

"Of course, he's the young man with the sexual orientation problem. I asked him to let us know how it played out, but this doesn't sound good."

"I never had a problem with my sexual orientation, so you're the one better able to advise him than I. Stay close to your cell phone tomorrow in case I need you," Roger requested.

"Will do!" Jimmy promised, and he kissed Roger softly on the lips.

That night as they prepared for bed, and before making love, they offered their private prayer to God. This time they added a little wish for Matthew's well-being.

At precisely 10 AM the next morning there was a knock on Roger's door. Matthew did not look familiar to him at all. Roger knew that there were always people at the service who ran out quickly, just as it was concluding. They never waited to shake hands with the minister. He could not fathom why they needed to maintain such anonymity.

The two men shook hands and Roger beckoned him to a chair facing his desk. As soon as Matthew was seated, Roger smiled at him as if to say, "You can begin now," but Matthew remained silent so Roger said, "Pastor Winningham filled me in on your conversation with him. Are you still hanging out with your friend?"

"Yes." Matthew grew silent again.

"And?" Roger asked.

"He tells me he loves me and wants to have sex with me."

"How do you feel about him?"

"I'm confused. I think about him all the time, but I don't think I could have sex with him."

"Then you must be straight," Roger averred.

"I don't know. I had an opportunity to have sex with my sister's girlfriend the other night, and I ran away. I didn't think I could get aroused, and she's really beautiful."

"Gee Matt, it sounds to me like you are a virgin, and probably need a sex therapist, not me."

"I know, and I intend to go if necessary, but I wanted to ask you a few questions first."

"I'll try to answer them as honestly as I can," Roger said reassuringly. Silently he asked Robbie to show up and guide him.

"Did you ever have doubts about your sexuality?" Matthew asked.

"No."

"Did you ever have fears about sleeping with a male?"

"Of course, but it didn't stop me. I actively sought out men to sleep with. I went to the bars. Finally I met a nice guy and lost my virginity."

"Did you ever want to sleep with a woman?"

"Not really. I admit to being curious, but I have never done it. Look, my partner had all kinds of confusion with his sexual orientation, but when we met, he couldn't wait to jump into bed with me. He was confused and scared, but he wanted to do it, and he did. Maybe you just don't have strong enough feelings for your friend."

"Maybe that's it."

"Have you ever met a man or a woman that you did desire to have sex with?" Roger asked the question this time.

"Oh yes."

"Was it a man or a woman?"

"A man!"

"There you go," Roger said. "You must be gay. Was the man gay? Did you ever tell him how you felt?"

"He was gay and I never told him."

"Maybe you should tell him."

"He has a partner. I'm afraid, he would reject me."

"My partner and I are monogamous, but there are many gay couples who have an open relationship. Do you know if he's monogamous?"

"Yes, he is."

"How do you know?"

"He just told me."

Roger was stunned. In fact he was speechless. His mind was working overtime. If this could happen to him, imagine how many gay men could fall in love with Jimmy in the gay church. Roger was actually shaking, but he felt Robbie's presence reassuring him. *You can handle this.*

He went over to Matthew and put his arms around him. "Matthew," he said, "This sounds bad, but it's really good. We have learned so much."

"What have we learned?" Matthew asked. "That I love you?"

"No, that you think you love me. My boy, the important thing that we have learned is that you are gay. It's not uncommon to think you are in love with your doctor, your teacher, or your minister. It's puppy love, and you must move on. I'm not available, but your friend is, and he's in love with you. Give him a break. At your age you have strong sexual urges. Let your friend satisfy them. Once you have made love with him, you'll see how much you two care for each other."

"Are you advising me to have sex with my friend?" Matthew asked.

"Not at all. I am advising you to make love with him if you want to. You can have sex with anyone, but you only make love to a special someone."

"I'm sorry I embarrassed you," Matthew said.

"You didn't embarrass me, but I want you to stay in touch with me and let me know what happens. I also want you to greet me and shake my hand after services. Promise? Does your friend attend church with you?"

"No, he goes to the gay church and has been urging me to go there. I kept saying no because I needed to see you and I wasn't sure I was gay."

"I think it would be a good idea if you did go there," Roger said sincerely. "My feelings would not be hurt. It might be good for you not to see me for a while and attending church together might bring you and your friend closer together."

"Do you know the minister there? Is he as wise and compassionate as you?"

"Yes, I know the pastor and the assistant pastor there, and they are both very wise and compassionate."

Matthew rose slowly from his chair, and Roger expected a handshake but the lad ran from Roger's office without saying another word.

When Matthew was gone, Roger slumped in his chair. He knew he couldn't do another stitch of work that day, and he was grateful that his sermon for tomorrow was written, edited and approved by Jimmy. They had taken to advising each other on their sermons.

He knew that Jimmy would still be in his office, but he rushed home and decided to make lunch for the two of them. He called Jimmy just to make sure that he was available for lunch. Jimmy answered and assured him that he would be home within the hour.

Roger's brain was working overtime. He was in turmoil. Then he remembered something. He called his college friend, Alex, who taught high school social studies. Alex's wife answered, and after a few words of greeting, she put Alex on.

Without any preliminaries, Roger asked, "How do you handle students who get a crush on you?"

"Are you nuts?" Alex asked. "I ignore it. The crush always passes."

"What if they come and tell you that they have a crush on you?"

"I tell them that this is inappropriate behavior, and I am going to report them to their parents and the principal."

"You're no help," Roger informed Alex.

"Why not?"

"One of my congregants has a crush on me. He told me so. Because of that, he can't pursue a relationship with his boyfriend. He's of legal age, and I can't report him to anyone."

"Have bad sex with him. He'll appreciate his boyfriend," Alex joked.

"That won't work either. He has never had sex with his boyfriend or anyone else so he can't compare."

"Then send him to a sex therapist," Alex advised.

"I've already recommended that to him."

"Then ask Jimmy for advice. Something like this should be right up his alley."

"You're right," Roger said. "And guess what? The boyfriend goes to Jimmy's church."

"OY!" Alex groaned and hung up.

When Jimmy got home, Roger did not hesitate to lay out the whole dilemma. All Jimmy could say is, "I wonder which of my guys it is?"

"That's not helpful," Roger said.

"I know. Let's discuss the problem over lunch. For what it's worth I've got a crush on you too." Jimmy gave Roger a crushing bear hug. They both heard Robbie laughing.

Stop laughing and help us out here, Roger thought, and he hoped Robbie got the message.

Chapter Seven

Several weeks went by and Roger did not hear from Matthew. He searched for his face among his congregation, but he never saw him. Christine, who managed the church office, kept the records of donations for income tax purposes. Roger enlisted her help and they found seven Matthews. Roger knew them all. He resigned himself to the realization that he would probably never hear from Matt again.

Then one afternoon there was a knock on Jimmy's office door. "Come in," he said automatically. A young man walked in. He smiled disarmingly at Jimmy.

"What can I do for you?" the pastor asked.

"I'm relatively new here," the man said. "I've been coming for the past few Sundays with my boyfriend. I used to go to St Benedict Episcopal, and someone just happened to mention to me the other day that you and Father Graham were partners."

"Yes we are. Do you know Roger?"

"Intimately. You stole him from me, you bastard." The deranged Matthew whipped out a pistol, aimed it directly at Jimmy's chest and fired point blank before Jimmy could react. Then he took the gun, placed it to his temple and shot himself.

Jimmy felt a strange vibration in his chest. He felt as if he was disintegrating. He was getting light headed, and was somehow floating in air. He looked down and could see Matthew lying in a pool of blood. Indistinctly he could see another person lying close by, but he couldn't tell who it was, or if he even knew the man.

He became aware that someone was calling his name. He looked up and there in front of him was Robbie. They grabbed each other and embraced. Robbie was crying. "It wasn't supposed to happen like this. You were supposed to have a long and happy life. I wasn't supposed to lose my heart twice."

"I know," Jimmy said. "You promised me years of happiness with Roger."

"Nothing like this was supposed to happen," Robbie wailed. They held each other tightly trying to comfort one another. Suddenly Jimmy was ripped from Robbie's arms and everything went black.

When Darryl heard gunshots coming from Jimmy's office, He ran toward the sounds without thinking that he might be in danger himself. He threw open Jimmy's door, stopped dead in his tracks and gasped. Trying to avoid all the blood, he ran to Jimmy's desk and called 911.

At the precise moment that Jimmy was shot, Roger was dictating a letter to Ellie. Suddenly he felt like he had been stabbed in his chest and he let out a shriek. He looked down fully expecting to see blood all over.

"What's the matter?" Ellie screamed.

"I don't know. I'm OK now, but I got this pain in my chest."

Heart attack, Ellie thought. She ran to her desk and got two aspirins. She made Roger swallow them over his objections. As he was downing the aspirins, he heard Robbie telling him to go to Jimmy.

He has rejected Robbie's heart, was all he could think. Without heed to Ellie he ran out to the parking lot, got his car, and headed for Jimmy's church. He drove recklessly, but he got there without incident. The area around the church was blocked off by a slew of police cars. He was unable to drive in to the church parking lot, but he saw an ambulance speeding away. Roger instinctively followed the ambulance to the hospital. They went to the very hospital where Jimmy had received his transplant.

At the emergency room entrance the paramedics unloaded a gurney and rushed into the ER. Roger parked and followed them in. He assumed it was Jimmy. He had never gone into the church to check. A team of hospital personnel were working on the man on the gurney. Roger could not get close. He tried to get the patient's name, but for the moment he was admitted as John Doe.

Roger wisely called the church and asked for Darryl. The switchboard did not want to put him through, but when he told them who he was, they connected his call.

A weeping hysterical Darryl was on the other end of the line. Between bitter sobs, Roger learned that a young man had entered Jimmy's office, shot Jimmy, and then shot himself. Jimmy was barely alive and was taken to the hospital. The police took the murderer away in a body bag, and as of now Darryl didn't know who he was.

Roger went to the nurse's station in the ER. The nurses recognized him immediately. "Good morning Father Graham," one of them said. "Can I help you?"

"Yes, the man who they just brought in, the one who was shot, he's a fellow clergyman. He has no family at all. His church family is all he has. Can you get me any information? We're like brothers."

The compassionate nurse told Roger to have a seat and promised to find out what she could. "Thank you," Roger said and broke out crying.

"They just took him into the OR. I'll check on him for you," she said. Before she went into the OR, the nurse got Roger a cup of water.

It seemed forever, but it was only a few minutes when the nurse returned. "Your friend had a heart transplant here several months ago." Roger nodded. "He's very lucky," she continued. "The bullet missed the heart by a hairline, but his left lung was punctured. He's in the OR now. The doctors are trying to repair the lung. If he survives the operation it will be a few days before we'll know what his chances are. He was shot at very close range and he lost a lot of blood."

"Thank you," Roger said, as the tears flowed again. The staff asked him to please wait in the hospital lobby, because the ER tended to get pretty hectic at night and it was getting late.

He sat in the lobby waiting for the operation to be over and for some more news. He was praying hard when someone called his name. He looked up to see Peter. "I was just passing through the lobby to go home and I saw you. What's happened?"

Peter sat down next to Roger. His horror grew as he heard the story. "How come Ellie didn't call me?" He asked nobody in particular.

"God, I never called her back." Roger got on his phone and Ellie answered immediately.

"You had me worried sick," she complained. When Roger filled her in on the shooting, they both started to cry so hard that Peter took the phone.

"I'll stay with Roger," he told Ellie. Why don't you come down here as soon as you can? We shouldn't leave him alone."

The words weren't out of his mouth when Darryl and William showed up. They tried unsuccessfully to comfort Roger and finally they decided to leave, since there was nothing they could do here. They made Roger promise to call as soon as he knew something.

Ellie showed up about a half hour later. She and Peter never left Roger's side. He had no appetite, but they made him drink juice or coffee, whatever they could get down him.

Rabbi Joe was making his late afternoon rounds when he heard the news. He rushed down to the lobby and found Roger. He threw his arms around him and rocked him gently as Roger sobbed against his chest.

"Don't lose faith," he said. "We are all praying."

Shortly after Joe left, Peter went to find out what he could. He came back in a few minutes. "The operation just ended and they are taking Jimmy to ICU. The doctor will be out shortly to speak to us."

The doctor recognized Roger immediately as one of the hospital chaplains. He also knew that Jimmy and Roger were life partners and he determined to treat Roger as a blood relative, and ignore hospital privacy policies which allowed only blood relatives to receive news about or to visit a patient in ICU.

"The good news is that he survived a very delicate and complicated surgery. It will be at least 48 hours before we'll know what his chances are. If he's a fighter, I believe he has a better than even chance to make it. Is he a fighter, Roger?"

"You bet he is," Roger said slightly relieved.

"There are some policemen in ICU. They want to question him as soon as he wakes up. They won't let anyone stay with him until they interview him, so why don't you go home. I'll leave orders to call you if necessary."

"Thanks doctor. I think I'll just hang out here."

"You can stay with me tonight," Peter said. You shouldn't be alone."

"Please everybody, I appreciate your concern, but I really would like to camp out in the hospital tonight. I promise to keep busy. I'll make my rounds in the morning."

Finally everyone gave into his wishes. Roger settled into the most comfortable chair he could find in the lobby. He called Darryl and brought him up to date. Before hanging up Darryl asked him to stay with him as well, but he declined.

Just before midnight, a young man came running into the lobby. He went to the information desk and the women at the desk pointed at Roger. The young man hurried over to Roger.

"Father Graham?" he asked.

"Yes. Do I know you?"

"No, but I think you know of me. My name is Ira Lawrence. I am, I was, Matthew's friend. I am so sorry for what happened. Had I been smarter, I might have prevented it."

Roger put his hand on the young man's shoulder. "How could you have prevented it?" he wanted to know.

"When I met Matt, I immediately fell in love with him. He was so shy that I found it appealing. I tried to get him to open up, but it was useless. We went out a lot and I tried to maneuver him into bed, but he kept insisting that he wasn't gay, which was pure bullshit. My gaydar never lies.

"One day he told me that he had a long talk with his minister and that now he thought he might be gay after all. He said that you advised him to go to the gay church with me. I actually hoped that now, he would go to bed with me, but he kept on resisting my pleas.

"Last Sunday after church a few of us were in the social hall having a cup of coffee. Matt mentioned that he used to go to St Benedict. One of the guys asked if he knew you. He said he did.

"The guy then asked if he knew that Pastor Jimmy and Father Roger were life partners. He never answered. He just leered at all of us and ran out of the hall. He was acting like a crazy man. I could see it, but I didn't think it would lead to anything as violent as this. I also attributed his virginity and his inward personality to his being shy, but now I can see how sick he was. God, Father, I feel so guilty for not telling anyone. I am so sorry."

Ira began to cry. Roger put his arms around him to console him. "Go home now, Ira," Roger said. "You could not have known what would happen or prevented it from happening. Don't let this ruin your life. I am making it an order. Go in peace and pray for your pastor's life."

Ira kissed Roger on the lips and ran from the lobby. Roger fell asleep, and slept for three hours from sheer exhaustion. In the morning, his position allowed him to wander freely through the hospital. He found an empty room, where he showered, but he had to put on the same clothes. He knew he would have to go home for a brief while to change, but he wasn't going to leave until Jimmy woke up. He went to the cardiac ward where Peter worked and found his friend.

"Can you tell me anything? Is there any news?" Roger asked.

"Yes, I was looking for you. Jimmy woke up about an hour ago. The cops are questioning him now and then he is being transferred to the surgical floor. Unfortunately, I won't be his nurse, but I promise to look in on him."

"How is his condition?" Roger asked.

"Serious, but stable. He's not out of danger, but they are watching him very closely." That didn't sound too bad, and Roger allowed himself to breathe.

"Can I hang out in the lobby until they bring him to his bed?"

"You can, but he won't be there for two or three hours. Why don't you go home, freshen up, and by the time you get back, he might be there."

That made sense to Roger, and he told Peter he would see him later. On the way home, he stopped at his church. He knelt before the altar and prayed like he had never prayed before. He felt something at his side and he knew that it was Robbie, who was praying also.

Chapter Eight

When the police left, Jimmy fell asleep again. When he awakened, his first sight was of Roger smiling broadly at him. Robbie was standing behind him looking very concerned. Jimmy tried to talk, but he had tubes going down his throat and speech eluded him.

"Bummer," he mouthed, and Roger smiled.

"That's an understatement," Roger responded. "Don't try to talk. Leave it to me. It seems that my not so secret admirer blamed you for his lack of success in nabbing me. In case you are wondering, he shot himself in the head after he shot you and we've lost him. His boyfriend came to console me. His name is Ira Lawrence. Do you know him?"

Jimmy shook his head to indicate that he did not know the young man.

"Ira wanted to apologize to me for missing all of Matt's symptoms. I ended up by consoling him."

Somehow Jimmy found Roger's hand and squeezed it. With that small action he assured Roger that he would be all right. Even Robbie's glum face put on a smile. Just then Joe came into the room. He embraced Roger and bent over Jimmy. Joe ran his fingers through Jimmy's hair. "You're

going to make it, buddy," he said. "God is with you. Would you mind if I
say a little prayer for you?"

Jimmy nodded, and Joe started to say his prayer in Hebrew. Much to
Jimmy's surprise, Robbie joined in. Nobody in that room, at that moment,
doubted that Jimmy would survive and be restored to full health. Robbie
even whispered in his ear that *their* heart was functioning just fine.

"You can all come back later," a voice said. "I need to bathe this guy,
put on a new gown, and change his IV. Y'all get something to eat in the
meantime." It was Mandy, who had been Jimmy's night nurse after his
transplant. Jimmy smiled at her and she looked at him in mock disgust.

"Pastor Winningham, what is so wonderful about this hospital that you can't
stay away?" Fortunately she did not expect an answer.

Every day Jimmy got stronger. The doctors were amazed at the speed of
his recovery. Roger and Joe joked with the doctors. "That's because you
guys never factor God into the equation." The doctors, of course, ignored
the two clergymen.

By the end of the first week all the drainage tubes and IV's were removed and
Jimmy was back on solid foods. After ten days, the stitches were removed
and Jimmy was informed he could leave the hospital. He was elated, but
a little bit sad. This stay in the hospital had been totally different from his
first stay. This time his room was constantly filled with visitors. Most of his
congregation came to see him and wish him well. They favored kissing him
over handshakes and embraces. They prayed for him and with him. Mostly
Peter, Joe, Darryl, William, and Roger came to see him after visiting hours,
or they would never have been able to have a proper visit. Robbie never
left his side.

The morning after his stitches were removed, Mandy helped Jimmy get his
stuff together. Roger was coming to take him home

That first day when Jimmy came home, Roger did not go to work. He
undressed and lay down next to Jimmy in bed.

"Is everything working all right?" Roger asked.

"Jimmy removed the covers and said, "Look for yourself." Roger looked at Jimmy's very hard cock.

"Do you think…?" Roger started to ask.

"I think that if I sit up in bed and drop my legs over the side, I should have no trouble sucking you dry. On the other hand, I'm sure you can take care of me while I am flat on my back."

"Well, let's see how we can work things out," Roger said, as he leaned over and took Jimmy inside his waiting mouth.

That night the two lovers slept entwined. Their naked bodies were fused together and an angel guarded their bed. All was well with the world and there was peace on earth.

Three weeks later Jimmy was back at work. As he approached his pulpit on the first Sunday of his return, the congregation broke out into wild applause. Jimmy beamed. He could not remember a time when he had been so happy. Jimmy always conducted the first service, but he always stayed for the second. At the conclusion of the second service, he joined the crowd in the social hall before meeting Roger for lunch. He considered most of his flock to be friends, and he was not shy about kissing them when he greeted them. Every so often he would think back to the way he was, and he would shudder.

This day a young man approached him and asked if he could speak to him privately for just a moment. He promised not to keep him long. Jimmy took his arm and walked him over to a quiet corner of the room.

"I'm Ira Lawrence," he said. He was about to explain who he was, but Jimmy stopped him.

"My partner told me all about your little talk. There is no need to apologize. There was no way for you to know. Roger and I both spoke to him and we didn't have an inkling that he was violent and suicidal. Promise me you'll put all this behind you, and seek a healthy and fulfilling relationship."

With that the two men embraced.

"See that good looking guy talking to Pastor Darryl?" Ira asked. "We've kinda been seeing each other and it's looking good."

"I haven't seen him here before."

"He just started coming because of me. Let's go over there and I'll introduce you."

The two men approached Darryl and Ira's friend just as Darryl was leaving. Jimmy thought that there was something vaguely familiar about the young man.

"Josh, I'd like you to meet Pastor Jimmy. He usually delivers the homily at the first service so we haven't really met him."

"Nice to meet you Josh," Jimmy said. He no longer offered his hand. Now every newcomer got a hug. Josh hugged him right back. Just to make small talk, Jimmy asked, "Are you from Atlanta, Josh?"

"I've been living here for about 2 years. I go to Emory with Ira. I couldn't wait to get out of Arborville." Jimmy's face went ashen.

"Are you from Arborville, Josh? I used to have a congregation there."

"However could you stand it? The minister at my church spewed hatred against everyone, but especially gays. I couldn't wait to get out of there."

Jimmy thought *so that's why he looks familiar.*

"Josh, what's your family name?"

"Sommers. Why do you ask?"

Jimmy's knees almost gave out. Josh was Dan Sommers' boy. Once again he was filled with shame. Dan and Josh abided his venomous sermons and never said a word.

"Josh," he said. "I'm going to lay it on the line. I'm Pastor Winningham. I'm the jerk who ranted and raved and preached such hate, but I have changed a million percent, as you can see."

"My God. I didn't recognize you at all," Josh gasped.

"Tell me does Dan, er, your father, know that you are gay?"

"Oh sure. My dad and my cousin Mark are the greatest guys in the world and my biggest supporters. They and my Uncle Paul, who is gay, all helped me through my coming out. I couldn't love them more, and I can't wait for them to meet Ira. We are going home next weekend."

"Josh, your dad and cousin Mark are friends of mine. "Would it be all right if I called them and told them that I met you and you are attending my church? I know they will be pleased."

"I'll be speaking to my dad tonight. Can I tell him?"

"You bet, and when you get back from Arborville, if you two can get yourselves out of bed early enough, try the first service and see how I've changed. Hey I've got to go now and meet my other half."

Ira and Josh both hugged Jimmy so hard that his healing incisions hurt, but he said nothing. As they left, Josh kissed him on the cheek and said, "Pastor, I wouldn't have recognized you if my life depended on it. I hated you once, but now running into you has been a joyful miracle. You've made me real happy. Thank you so much."

As the boys ran off smiling and waving back at him, Jimmy thought, *Wait until Roger asks me if anything interesting happened in church today.*

That evening about 8 PM, the phone rang and Roger answered. "It's really nice to speak to you guys. I hope nothing is wrong and everyone is well."

Jimmy looked at him quizzically. "It's for you," Roger said, handing Jimmy the phone. It's Mark and Dan Sommers on a conference call."

"Hi fellas," Jimmy said jovially. "I surmise that you just spoke to Josh. All those years in Arborville, how could I not know what a great kid he was?"

"Maybe it's because you had a closed heart," Mark said, and laughed as he said it so that Jimmy would not take it wrong."

"I am so happy, Jimmy that you will be my son's minister, but tell me confidentially. I am so curious. What is his Ira like?"

"You will love him, mainly because he has a good heart. Beyond that, he's a student at Emory, he's very good looking, about 5'10" tall, blue eyes, dark brown hair, and when he looks at Josh, you can see all the love coming out of him. They are both good kids. They may not end up together, but if they do, it will be a very good thing. Roger has met Ira, but he hasn't met Josh yet. I intend to remedy all that by inviting them both to dinner real soon."

"Thank you so much for looking after my boy, but please tell me how you are doing."

"I'm just great. My heart is serving me well, and I am healing nicely from the lung surgery. Prior to the incident, Roger and I had both spoken to the kid who shot me, but unfortunately neither of us detected any symptoms of mental illness in him. We both simply believed he had a crush on Roger and that it was nothing more than puppy love. Be that as it may, it's in the past."

"Yes, thank God," Mark said. "All's well that ends well."

Roger and Jimmy were very engrossed in their work. They were available to serve their flocks 24-7, but they always made time for each other. Roger felt that God had spared Jimmy twice so that they could spend this lifetimes together, and he was not about to piss away God's good work by ignoring Jimmy. They always made time for each other,

In bed at night, they melded into one body. In a short time, it was not necessary to make love in awkward positions due to Jimmy's surgery. They were able to resume the physical aspect of their union without worrying about pulling, stretching or damaging any body parts. They made love often and with passionate abandon. Jimmy seemed determined to make up for 38 years of celibacy, and Roger seemed determined to help him in his quest.

Each man believed that his calling to the ministry was divinely inspired and they could not be happier in their work. The very fact that they were doing the same work bound them even closer, and since they were doing it separately, they never got in each other's way. Gay men and women felt just as accepted in Roger's church as they did in Jimmy's. There was no conflict there.

They shared a guardian angel. Robbie was an ever present entity. If they listened hard they could hear him and then they could heed his advice. When Robbie told Jimmy to take a few hours off to rest, he listened because Robbie was looking after their heart.

Rabbi Joe presided over an interfaith service at least once a year. Now that he knew Jimmy, he invited Darryl and Jimmy to participate. The other clergy of the area had absolutely no objections.

The service was always a celebration of love and good will. Roger and Jimmy were particularly happy to be conducting a service together, and with their good friend Rabbi Joe.

One beautiful spring day, Ira and Josh asked Jimmy to perform a commitment ceremony for them. It was a first for him, and he was especially thrilled because he knew the family of one of the participants.

Dan and his wife, Mary, attended, as well as Mark, his wife Jennifer, and their two children. Josh's Uncle Paul attended with his partner.

Ira's family was small. He had only a mother and a teen age sister. They were there too.

Darryl, William, Roger, and several close friends of Ira and Josh rounded out the guest list, but the church was full of most of the congregation.

Ira and Josh exchanged vows they had written for each other, and as they did, Jimmy and Roger looked into each other's eyes and smiled knowingly. Jimmy began to cry as he begged the boys to love each other always, take care of each other always, and never to forget that their union was made in heaven.

The parents made a reception in the social hall after the ceremony for the invited guests. There was a lot of love and joy in the church that day.

Before he left, Dan came over to Jimmy. "A year ago," he said, "if someone had told me that you would preside over the commitment ceremony of my son, I would have called the loony bin to come and take him away. I have seen a modern miracle, and now I can really relate to the expression, *God moves in mysterious ways.*

"Yes," Jimmy agreed. "It is a miracle and it is mysterious. I got a new heart and a new life, and I thank God and Robbie Cutler for it every day. Once upon a time I could not have dreamed that I could love anyone as strongly as I do and that he would love me back even more. I wasn't born with this heart, but I have adopted it and it's mine. It has given me the capacity to love, to forgive, to be charitable and to serve my fellow man. What else can a man ask out of life?"

That night as they were preparing for bed, Roger said, "I heard what you said to Dan. It was beautiful and I started to cry."

"I meant every word," Jimmy said, "especially about loving you."

Suddenly they were startled by a bright light shining in the room and the voice that had been guiding them said, *You two are going to be just fine. I think I can leave you now.*

Each felt Robbie's kiss on their cheeks. They wanted to cry, but before they could, Robbie put them into a deep and peaceful sleep.

ETERNAL LOVE

Chapter One

The young hustler sat at the bar, casting his eyes around the room, looking for a prospective customer. He was only eighteen, but he had a masterfully forged driver's license which said that he was nineteen. He was very good at spotting a likely candidate.

The man would be in his thirties or early forties, slightly overweight, usually beginning to bald. There would be a pale circle on his ring finger from where he had removed his wedding band. If the subject was new at this, he would be looking nervously around. If he was experienced he could easily spot the hustler at the bar, and he would approach the boy. Some of them would offer to buy him a drink; others would come right out and ask him, "How much?"

He was prepared for that. The boy had actually typed up a menu. It contained a list of sexual acts that he would perform on his customer, or that the customer could perform on him. Next to each activity was the price he charged. Also, in bold letters at the bottom of the menu, he had typed a message explaining that the customer could buy his services for the entire night for an **ADDITIONAL** $250. He rarely got an overnight customer because most of his clients were married. Occasionally an out of town business man took him back to his hotel and he collected a big fee for the night.

He had been hustling for almost four years now. As a boy he lived in a middle class neighborhood in St. Louis with his parents and his uncle. The boy's uncle was only two years older than he, and was being raised by the boy's father and mother.

One day his father came home from work early and found the two boys enjoying a hot game of sixty-nine. He kicked them both out of the house, leaving two teen aged boys to fend for themselves. At sixteen, his uncle was able to get a job at a Burger King in a nearby town, but he decided to ride the rails to Los Angeles and West Hollywood. He had heard lots about the gay life there. Once there, he began to work the bars. He actually made a good living, and because he looked older than he was, he convinced a prospective landlord to rent him a small studio apartment. He completely lost contact with his family in St. Louis including his uncle.

He had been in the bar for almost a half hour and had not yet spotted a likely candidate. He was 'cruised' by several hot looking guys but he gave them the brush off. He was completely caught off guard by what happened next.

He looked up to see a man standing in front of him. He had noticed every last person in the bar, but had not seen this dude before. Where did he come from? No matter, the boy was mesmerized. The man standing before him was a Greek God. He appeared to be about twenty years old, but at the same time, he appeared to be ancient. He stood 6'2" tall. His hair was long and straight, and the man tied it in a ponytail which came down below his shoulder blades. His eyes were jet black. His lips were blood red, but you could see that it was his natural color and not make-up. There was not an ounce of fat on him, yet he was not particularly muscular, just lean. He was wearing jeans, a tee shirt and floppies. But what was so striking about him was his complexion. He was so white you could see his veins, and his eyelashes were so long and black against his white skin, that the boy thought he was the most beautiful man he had ever seen.

The man looked at the person sitting on the bar stool next to the boy, and immediately that person picked up his drink and vacated his seat, relinquishing it to the handsome stranger.

"Would you like a fresh drink?" the man asked the boy. As he asked he put his hand on the boy's arm. His touch was ice cold to the boy, and at the same time it felt as if the man's hand was burning through his skin. He sensed that he should have felt pain, but the man's touch was strangely sensual. He also wondered where the man was from. He spoke English with some sort of accent.

"Sure," he answered.

Nothing more was said until the bartender put the boy's drink down in front of him. The drink was almost pure soda water. The bartender knew that when a hustler accepted a drink from a John, they really did not want to drink and get drunk. They needed to have their wits about them.

"Aren't you going to have a drink?" the boy asked.

"No, I don't drink," the beautiful, strange man answered. He let the boy take a few sips and then he asked him, "If I were to take you with me on a trip around the world, who would miss you?"

"Nobody," the boy answered, "but who says I would go with you?"

"It was just a hypothetical question. If that were to happen, who would we have to inform about your whereabouts?"

"Nobody," the boy answered more emphatically. "Why are you asking me these questions?"

The man didn't answer, but his black eyes peered intently into the boy's soft brown eyes. The boy was mesmerized. Suddenly he knew that he wanted to be with this man, to explore his body with his tongue and drink the man's juices. He knew instinctively that he could not charge this man for his services. He also knew that no matter what he did, this man would never be satisfied. It was deflating to the boy to realize that he had met a man he could never satisfy, or so he thought.

The man took the boy's hand and said, "Come with me." He led the boy out of the bar. They walked hand in hand for several streets. As they walked, the neighborhood grew darker and seedier. If the boy had not been following the man in a nearly comatose state he would have been frightened. The man led him down a dark alley. They reached a steel door and the man peered at the door, which opened and then closed without his touching it. The door led into a beautiful room, totally different than what you would expect in this neighborhood. There was a large king sized bed with plush pillows, beautiful sky blue linens and a comforter. The walls of the room were painted the same sky blue as the linens. There was a night stand with a lamp next to the bed and a dresser on the opposite wall. There were no windows in the room.

The lamp on the night stand had a blue shade so the dim light it emitted was a soft blue as well. Without speaking, the man's eyes commanded the boy to disrobe. The boy obeyed, and at the same time the man disrobed. They stood facing each other completely naked. They each reached out and took each other's cocks in their hands. The boy got immediately hard, but the man did not.

The boy fondled and coddled the man's cock. It was eerily cold, yet like the man's touch, it seared his palm. Finally the man began to erect. The boy wanted to fall to his knees and take the man's cock in his mouth, but somehow he was unable to move. Again the man looked at him. His eyes ordered him to lie down on the bed. The boy did as he was bid, lying on his back, legs spread and cock pointing to the ceiling. The man climbed on the bed and lay on top of the boy. The boy marveled that he felt no weight. The man was as light as a feather.

The strange man put his lips on the boy's and forced them open with his tongue. The boy was happy to oblige, but suddenly he turned his head away. The man's saliva had a strange and bitter taste. He had never tasted anything like it before. Unfortunately, when he tasted the saliva, he slipped even more from consciousness.

The man placed his mouth on the boy's neck. From some distant realm of near consciousness the boy thought that he would have one or more visible love bites in the morning. He could feel little pin pricks piercing his neck and he lost consciousness totally.

The man worked his way down the boy's body and reached his engorged cock. The cock was pulsing with blood. The man could hear it, see it and almost taste it. He could bear it no longer. All resistance left him and he bit into the engorged tool and sucked out all the blood. As he sucked he could feel his own orgasm approaching. He came in an ecstatic series of spasms, as the boy's penis became more and more flaccid. Suddenly, the man pulled himself up with a scream. The boy's blood had suddenly turned from pure honey and nectar into a bitter acrid solution, evidence that the boy was dead, and the strange man could never drink the blood of a dead person.

The man pulled the boy's corpse into his arms and held him tightly. "I'm sorry," he sobbed to the body. "I need to feed. I didn't want to kill you, but such is my life. I have no choice." He cried bitterly for some time, all the while rocking the boy's body in his arms. Finally he looked down. The body was covered with blood, his blood. His cum was blood and his tears were blood, and they covered the boy's body.

He wrapped the body in the bed linens so that no blood remained as evidence. Not bothering to dress, he lifted the body inside the bed sheets as if it had no weight at all and he left the room. He seemed to float rather than walk until he came to a nearby crematorium. He went to the back door and it opened for him. He entered the facility and put the body down on the floor. The door of the crematorium oven opened at his command and he placed the body inside, linens and all. He closed the oven door and the fire ignited.

As he walked home, he was grateful that he would not have to feed for at least five more days. Before entering his lodgings, he stood in front of his door and sniffed the air. He detected nothing, and that saddened him even more. He was constantly sniffing the air, trying to detect another creature just like him. He yearned for a companion. His life was so lonely. He entered his room, and bolted the door behind him. He removed fresh linen from a dresser drawer and noted that after this set, there was only one left.

He made a mental note to shop for bed linen. He made up the bed and shut the dim blue light. He fell asleep quickly and did not wake for six days.

On the Friday evening following the hustler's death, Bookey (Booker) Stockwell jointly celebrated his eighteenth birthday and his senior prom. After the prom, he, his date and a few friends went back to his house. His mom had made a delicious birthday cake, which she served with coffee, tea and soda pop. His friends had brought gifts with them and after Bookey opened them, they left one couple at a time, until he was left alone with his date. His parents had gone to bed some time ago.

The two young graduates got into Bookey's father's car. "Let's go to Mulholland Drive before you take me home," she said. "After all," she continued, "it's prom night." She reached over and laid her hand on Bookey's crotch.

Bookey had been dreading this moment for months. Prom night was when young people traditionally lost their virginity, especially if they were sweethearts. The young man had no idea how he would get through this. Bookey had known for years that he was gay, but had done everything he could to hide the fact. He became a real high school jock, playing quarterback for the football team and pitching for the baseball team. He avoided dating one girl and opted for as many girls as possible, not letting anyone of them get the wrong idea.

He knew that if he was to preserve his secret he needed to fuck his date. They drove silently to a parking area on the drive. The girl rubbed her hand up and down Bookey's inner thigh during the entire trip. It was prom night after all, and Bookey could not find a place to park.

"I guess we'll have to leave," he said, but the girl spied a spot way at the end of the observation area and urged him to park there. As soon as Bookey turned off the ignition and shut the lights, she was all over him. She made him get into the back of the car. There, she grabbed at his cock and tried to zip open his pants. Bookey knew that he had to do something quickly.

He undid the cummerbund of his rented tuxedo, and helped her unzip his fly. He took out his still limp cock and placed it into her waiting palm. He started to kiss her, and he put his hand on her breasts. Finally he conjured up the vision of the man who always occupied his masturbation fantasies.

His fantasy lover was named Ernesto. He was tall and lean and not too muscular. His straight black hair was long and tied back in a ponytail. His long black eyelashes accentuated his alabaster skin. His eyes were mysterious and jet black. His lips were rose red and he fantasized kissing them. He was lost in the man's arms and he was caressing the man's hard uncircumcised cock. Now his hardon was throbbing with desire. The girl climbed on top of him. She positioned his cock at the opening to her vagina and pushed down on his cock as he pushed up and entered her. She gave a little squeal as he broke her hymen.

"Are you all right?" he asked.

"Yes," she replied but aren't you going to put on a condom?"

He had grown so horny thinking about his dream man, that he had completely forgotten to use protection. He reached into his wallet and extracted a lubricated condom. She helped him put it on. He reentered her easily now and they began to fuck. He was dreaming that he was fucking the handsome stranger of his fantasies. They were lying naked in an open field in some distant, far away land. The place did not look much like California. The man was caressing his face, kissing him, and for some reason, he called him Johnny.

He came long before she did, but he had prepared for this moment and he knew what to do. He removed the condom and tossed it out the window. Then he laid his date down on the back seat and he went down on her. His tongue found her clitoris after a little while, and he began to run his tongue lightly over it while he dreamed he was sucking Ernesto's cock. He felt himself getting hard again as she began to moan and writhe with pleasure. In time her body began to spasm and she began to scream as she experienced the first orgasm that a man had ever given to her. Bookey kept sucking away and wasn't even aware that she came two more times before she made him stop.

She pulled him up to her and began to kiss him hard, then gently, and murmured in his ear, "You are fantastic."

She saw that he was hard again and she made him switch positions with her. Her tongue found his cock and she started to suck it just as she had fantasized doing for years. He began to picture his fantasy lover sucking him off and he came again in no time. Much to his surprise, she swallowed his cum. She climbed up on top of him and said once again, "You are fantastic."

After a while they uncoupled and got dressed as best they could and Bookey took her home.

The beautiful strange man didn't usually dream, but there were rare occasions when he did. Just before he awakened from his six day hibernation he had a dream. Not only was this a rare thing to happen to him, but he remembered the dream in great detail.

He was sitting in the passenger side of a two year old Pontiac. A handsome young man was in the driver's seat. Somehow he knew that the car belonged to the young man's father. The two of them got out of the car intending to sit in the back. He looked at the beautiful young man. They were nothing alike. The young man was 6'4" tall, muscular and athletic. His blond hair was cut short in a buzz. His eyes were blue and when the young man looked at him, his gaze seemed to shine right through him.

They got into the back seat and locked the door. Then they started groping for each other's cocks and finally they were free of their clothing, and their erect cocks were out there for the taking. The young man's cock was bigger and fatter than his. He laid himself on the back seat in a position to allow the young man to enter him. The young man began to do so, but stopped to put on a lubricated condom. He found that strange. The young man reached his climax quickly. He withdrew and ripped off the condom and immediately went down on him and brought him to orgasm three times. In his dream he gushed out real semen, not blood. In gratitude he went down on the young man and gave him another orgasm. They kissed and lay in each other's arms for a while and his dream ended. When he awoke a short time later he had to make himself believe that his dream wasn't real.

The night after the prom, Bookey vowed to really lose his virginity, with a man. It was Saturday night. His folks went out, but their friends had picked them up and his dad said he could use his car. He dressed as skimpily as he could; no underwear, short shorts, a tank top and sandals. His muscles bulged and rippled as he moved. He had been doing some spying and knew exactly where the gay section of town was, and where all the gay bars were. He drove there and paid to park in a ramp because he was unfamiliar with the neighborhood.

As he entered one of the bars, several hustlers gave him the eye, but they quickly rejected him as a possible client. This hunk needn't pay for anything. He found a seat at the bar, the very same one that the young hustler had sat in six nights ago. A dozen gorgeous young men approached him and asked to buy him a drink. "No," he said, "I'm waiting for someone." He had no idea why he said that. He came here to get laid. He wasn't waiting for anyone in particular. But after he said that for the fourth time, he gave the room a good looking over. There were some very good looking men out there, but nobody who made his cock jump. He wanted the first time to be very special.

Suddenly there he was. He was standing right in front of him, and it seemed as if he had come out of no place. Both men gasped.

"It's you!" they said in unison, and then they both started to laugh at the absurdity of it all.

"I have dreamed about you all my life," Bookey said. "Blindfold me and I'll draw you from memory, every line on your body and every blood vessel."

"I only dreamed about you for the first time a few hours ago," the strange man said, "but I would know you anywhere."

The two men fell into each other's arms and began to kiss. The strange man could smell the other's blood. He was hungry and he was frightened. He could never hurt this person. He loved him. He pushed Bookey aside and asked, "Will you trust me for about an hour? I have urgent business, but I don't want to lose you. Promise you'll be here when I get back."

The young man nodded.

"Please don't go off with any of these vultures. I swear I'll come back for you."

Bookey took the strange man's hand and put it on his crotch. The strange man felt Bookey's erect cock. "Does that feel like I'm going to go off without you?"

The strange man smiled and asked, "When you touch me, do I feel cold to you?"

"Why are you asking me that?" Bookey wanted to know. "You feel as warm as toast. Don't you know that I have loved you for years and years? I thought at first that you were a fantasy, but in time you became as real to me as my parents. I knew I would find you some day and I would be yours for all eternity."

"Eternity is a long time," the strange man said.

"It would be a second in time if I could spend it with you," Bookey said.

The strange man smiled and repeated, "Wait for me, please, I beg you."

Bookey nodded and said, "Before you go tell me your name."

"Ernest!" said the man, as he ran off.

Ernest ran up and down the streets in a state of euphoria. He had not loved anyone since his mortal days in Italy over three hundred years ago. He was Ernesto then and madly in love with Gianni. One day the parish priest, who was old and deformed, took the men to his room. He had somehow hypnotized or drugged both boys. First he drained Gianni of all his blood and then he turned Ernesto by exchanging blood with him. He forced Ernesto to be his lover.

Ernesto swore he would get revenge. The two men mostly slept during the day. When the priest needed to do church business during the day, or to serve mass, he kept the church very dark and returned immediately to his chambers. On one such occasion the priest rushed back to their room. He locked the door and went immediately to sleep. Ernesto was only pretending to be asleep. He got up quietly and removed a wooden stake from under his mattress. With one strong push he propelled the stake through the priest's heart. It was amazing. No blood flowed. The priest's body simply shriveled up and turned to dust. "Victory," Ernesto yelled. "This is for you my beloved Gianni."

Ernesto waited until dark. He took the linens containing the priest's remains and scattered the dust to the winds. He helped himself to the priest's stash and took a coach to France. A little over a hundred years later he sailed to America.

Now as Ernest, he prowled the streets looking for food so that he would not harm Bookey in his greed. Finally, he came across a homeless man sleeping against a dumpster in a dark, deserted alley. Malnutritioned subjects like this one did not have the best tasting blood, but he didn't care. He just wanted to feed and get back to Bookey.

When he returned to the bar, he found Bookey on the same barstool, nursing the same drink. He rushed up to him. The two men hesitated for only a second and fell into each other's arms. Ernest forgot himself and opened his lips offering Bookey his tongue. Their tongues caressed each other for a bit and Ernest realized that Bookey had not pulled away in disgust. He separated for a moment and he could see a little speckle of blood on Bookey's lips.

"Are you alright?" Ernest asked Bookey.

"Yes! Why do you always ask these strange questions?"

"How did I taste to you?"

Like sweet potato pie," Bookey answered and resumed kissing Ernest.

Ernest wanted to hypnotize Bookey and take him home with him, but he didn't want to force him. He was about to ask him to come home with him, when Bookey said, "Of course, I want to go home with you." Had Bookey read his mind? He tested his premise.

"I love you," he projected telepathically to Bookey.

"Bookey smiled back and said, "I love you too. It never occurred to him to communicate silently as Ernest had.

Ernest took Bookey's hand and they got his dad's car out of the parking ramp. They retraced the route Ernest had taken less than a week earlier with another young man. When Ernest's door opened and closed by itself, Bookey wasn't surprised. Since laying eyes on Ernest, nothing could surprise him.

Once inside the two men undressed. They stood facing each other and both had throbbing erections. They started out by playing sixty-nine and then Ernest begged Bookey to fuck him. "It's been a very long time," he said to Bookey.

"I know," Bookey responded. "More than three hundred years."

"How did you know?"

"I can read your mind just as you can read mine," Bookey answered. Suddenly he burst out laughing.

"What?" Ernest wanted to know.

"If we can read each other's minds we damn well better be faithful lovers. I'll fuck you after I suck you dry." Ernest panicked at the thought that Bookey might be revolted by his emissions of blood, but Bookey soothed him. "Don't be afraid. It will be fine, I promise."

Bookey went down on Ernest. It was the first time he had sucked cock, but Ernest kept thinking of what he would like done. Bookey read his mind and complied with his silent wishes. Ernest came, screaming loudly and gushing his blood down Bookey's throat. Bookey drank every drop, and collapsed in exhaustion next to Ernest.

"That tasted like honey," Bookey told Ernest. "Turn me," Bookey begged, "so I can shoot my blood up your ass and seal our union. I can't be separated from you ever, not for an instant."

Ernest jumped out of bed and got a knife from a cabinet. Before Bookey could say anything Ernest slit his wrist. "Drink," he said to Bookey, "before the skin heals itself." Bookey bent down and drank as much blood as he could, but the wound was healing fast.

"How will I know when I have turned?" Bookey asked.

Ernest turned Bookey's face toward the bedside lamp. "I am going to light it. Tell me what you see."

Ernest lit the lamp and Bookey recoiled. "It's too bright," he yelled. "Turn it off."

Ernest engulfed Bookey in his arms, hugging him as tight to him as he could. "You're mine now my dearest love. Fuck me and let's see what comes out of you."

They made love for hours, but then they got up and drove Bookey's dad's car back to his house before daylight could come.

"What should I do, love?" Bookey asked Ernest. "I can't just run out without an explanation. It's not fair to them.

"Leave them a note saying that you are going to visit a friend up in Canada using a rental car. Tell them you are going for the fishing. We'll go up to Canada and we'll abandon the car there.

Bookey's dad always left a pad and pencil in the glove compartment. Bookey wrote the note and left it in the car. They ran back to Ernest's place so quickly that they were a mere blur.

"We'll rent a car," Ernest said. "We'll abandon it just over the border in some deserted spot. Sooner or later someone will find it, but not your body. You'll be one of those persons who disappear without a trace. I'm sorry to put your parents through this, but you are really dead you know, and you have to burn all the old bridges, so you can start your new existence."

"I know my love. It was my choice. You didn't force me. Now kiss me and let's make love before we leave for Canada."

Chapter Two

They decided to take a nice slow drive up to Canada. By mutual consent they drove cross country and entered Canada on the Eastern side. Ernest said that it would be a sort of grand tour graduation present for Bookey. Of course, they drove only at night, checking in at attractive motels along the way, long before the dawn. They could see at night better than humans can see during the day so they were able to enjoy the sights along the way even though they slept during the day.

When they made love, they exchanged their blood so that in just a few days, Bookey had become as powerful a vampire as Ernest had become over three centuries.

During the trip, Ernest taught Bookey how to stalk his quarry and end his life quickly and painlessly. The teacher taught the student to try to limit his kill to pimps, prostitutes, and criminals. He cautioned him to read his victim's mind and if he was a family man or a man of good deeds he should not take his blood.

It took them almost two weeks of slow travelling to reach The Rainbow Bridge crossing into Canada at Niagara Falls, NY. Ernest rolled down the window for the immigration and custom's officer. The officer opened his mouth and looked at the two men. He was gay and his mind was trying to find a reason to take them inside and frisk them, but all he could do was to wave them on; no questions asked.

They drove about a mile into Canada. The road was dark and deserted. Ernest found an opening in the heavily tree lined highway and drove the car through the thicket. When it could go no more, the men exited the auto. Before leaving Los Angeles they had filled a back pack with the clothes Bookey had worn to the bar. Later they entered a men's clothing store after hours and outfitted themselves. All they had and all they needed was the clothes on their backs. They were capable of getting fresh clothing at their leisure.

They left the back pack in the car and abandoned it. They returned to the highway, and just a few yards up the road they saw a sign indicating that Toronto was 115 km ahead. They decided that they would spend a few days there before moving on to another destination. Ernest was determined to show Bookey the world and they had plenty of time to do it.

They smiled at each other and started to run, or it was more like gliding, up the highway. They stayed at the side of the road to avoid traffic and achieved speeds of about sixty miles an hour. They reached the city limits in a little under two hours. Neither was tired and the night was young. They decided to get a hotel room and then go out on the town, and feed before dawn.

When they entered the city limits, they saw a bus stop up ahead. It had a picture of the route the bus took and they saw that it terminated in downtown Toronto. They decided to take the bus and remain inconspicuous. The bus came along in about fifteen minutes. Ernest stared at the bus driver as they climbed aboard and he was oblivious to the fact that they didn't pay. One passenger thought she had seen these men not pay the fare, but she wasn't sure and she didn't care.

When they reached the downtown area, it was not yet eight o'clock. Their first stop was a luggage store where they chose two small suitcases. As they left the store, the proprietor smiled at them and said, "Thank you gentlemen. Come again, won't you." A few doors up the street, they found a men's furnishing shop. They helped themselves to whatever they thought they might need for a few days' stay and stuffed everything into their suitcases. Fortunately it was summer. Although they didn't need to wear clothing in any temperature, it would have looked crazy for them not to wear winter clothes if it was winter in Canada.

On the way out of the store they asked the proprietor to direct them to the nearest five star hotel. He did, and he also thanked them for shopping at his establishment. They took a cab to the hotel and as they exited the cab, the driver helped them with their suitcases and thanked them for their generosity. Ernest paid and tipped the man. Bookey wondered where the Canadian money had come from.

At the front desk, the clerk went through the motions of recording a non-existent credit card, and had one of the boys take them to their room. Ernest and Bookey knew immediately that the bell hop was gay, not because he was checking them out with lust, which he was, but because they could read his mind. He was a college student who worked long hours at night to pay for his tuition. They both liked him immediately and silently vowed no harm would come to him.

"Can you direct us to some gay hot spots in town, Larry?" Bookey asked, reading the bell hop's ID badge. Larry broke out into the widest grin either of them had ever seen. They immediately let him know telepathically that they were off limits to him. His grin shortened just a smidgen, but he was happy to name several good places and to give them directions. They were all within walking distance from each other and from the hotel. Ernest gave Larry a big tip.

When they were alone in the room, Bookey asked Ernest where he had gotten the Canadian money. "From an ATM machine," he answered. I pay my way to worthy people, but I hypnotize gougers. The owners of the luggage store, the clothing store, and the hotel all overcharge their customers. They won't miss what we took, but the cab driver and Larry are working hard to make their way in this world and they deserve payment." Bookey was busy trying to figure out when Ernest had used an ATM machine and he was unaware of it.

"I'm hungry," Bookey told Ernest. "Shall we feed before we party?"

"Capital idea," Ernest responded.

They removed all the labels and hung up their new clothes. They stashed the luggage in the closet, and left the hotel. In front of the hotel, Ernest stopped and sniffed the air. Bookey knew he was sniffing for prey. He was learning how to do it, but had not yet fully mastered the art.

"This way," Ernest said and smiled at his lover. He led Bookey up the street and turned into an alley. Out of the shadows a voice asked, "Do you dudes have stash for tonight?" It was a drug dealer.

"It depends what you are selling," Ernest answered. The drug dealer was totally unaware, but Ernest could see him pulling a knife out of his trouser belt. So fast, that no camera could have photographed it, Ernest had the man pinned against the concrete wall and his teeth were buried in the man's jugular.

Suddenly the dealer's accomplice dove out of nowhere and right at Bookey. Of course, Bookey had smelled him and he caught his assailant in midair. He pulled him toward him and sank his teeth into his jugular as well. For more than five minutes the two men drank their victims' blood until they each died and they had to stop feeding. Ernest took his assailant's knife and cut his neck up so that his teeth marks did not show. Then he did the same to Bookey's victim.

"Search your man for his stash," Ernest directed. They retrieved the stash and emptied the stuff all over the bodies.

"The police will think it was a drug related slaying. Now let's go have some fun."

Fully fed and able to resist the smell of blood from human beings, they went to a gay bar, and they did indeed have fun. They danced and carried on engagingly for the crowd. They even made two new friends who asked them to join them at a different bar the next evening and they gladly accepted. Another young man asked Ernest if his accent was Italian. When Ernest said that it was, the young man said that he had recently emigrated from Italy and was dying to speak Italian to someone. He and Ernest started speaking but the young man found Ernest's speech to be structured and clumsy. Ernest was speaking Old Italian in what can be compared to Shakespearean English as it would sound to a modern day English speaking man.

They stayed far into the night. They were not tired and knew that they would sleep all day. They were the last to leave the bar. As they walked slowly back to the hotel, they passed the alley where they had fed. It was lit up and cordoned off. The place was crawling with cops. Obviously the bodies had been discovered.

Bookey stopped in front of a cop. "What's going on, officer?" he asked innocently.

"Nothing that concerns you young man," the cop answered him. "Just move along, please." It struck Bookey that the cops tone was polite but firm. He wasn't nasty like a Los Angeles cop might have been in the circumstances. He had always heard from friends who had travelled to Canada that Canadians were a super polite people, and wherever they went, they were made to feel welcome. Bookey had to agree.

Back in the hotel, they put a "Do Not Disturb" sign on their door, and undressed and showered together. Both felt the need to cleanse themselves of the odor of the drug dealers. Once in bed, they held their bodies tightly together. Their fingers began to explore their partner's every erotic spot. By now they knew what thrilled them both. When they were dueling with their tongues, they took little nips of each other. Tiny droplets of blood invaded their mouths and intermingled. The tongues healed immediately but the taste of the blood went right to their groins. They nipped each other's nipples, achieving the same results. When they were sucking each other's cocks, they would also nip out little globules of blood and when they were fucking they would feed from each other's necks. They loved each other and would never harm one another. The droplets of blood were miniscule, but the effect on their libidos was gigantic. Sometimes they were so aroused that they would cum without either touching the other's cock. When that happened they scurried to drink up as much of the blood as possible and avoid a mess. They much preferred to cum in their mouths or up their asses. No blood was spilled and when they received each other's blood internally, there are no words to describe the ecstasy they felt. Drinking a criminal's blood was dinner. Drinking each other's blood was Nirvana.

That night after the love making, they made sure that the curtains and shades were drawn tight. They curled up together, intending to sleep that way through the day. Ernest was the first to speak. "I was so lonely. For three hundred years I looked all over for a lover companion. You were sent to me in a vision and I loved you before we met. Thank you for saving me from an eternity of loneliness."

"No, Ernesto, (Bookey loved to call Ernest by his real name when they were alone and intimate) it is I who must thank you. I hated my life. It was meaningless, except when I fantasized that you were my lover and we would be together forever. I have seen you, just as you are now, since I was thirteen. You saved me from a humdrum hateful life without you. Thank you for that, and for loving me as much as I love you. But please, I ask a favor of you. Don't love Gianni any less. Let us revere his memory together."

They kissed and absorbed a few droplets of blood from each other and slept until the next evening.

When they awoke they showered again to remove the odor of blood from their bodies. They wanted their breaths to smell fresh as well, so they brushed their teeth, which would never decay, and gargled with a breath freshener. They dressed in some of their new clothes, and discussed the need to feed before finding the gay bar where they were to meet their new friends. They both agreed that they felt no hunger and it was safe to mingle with good people and not put them in harm's way.

Before going down stairs, the two lovers embraced and kissed each other chastely. "Do you ever regret that I turned you?" Ernest asked.

Bookey smiled and answered. "Ernesto, Ernesto, sometimes I think you are the most sentimental fool I have ever met." He forced his tongue into

Ernest's mouth. Ernest instinctively took his droplets of blood. "Does that feel like regret? Anyway, you didn't turn me. I begged for it because I wanted to be with you forever. You will never be lonely again and I will never be unhappy. Furthermore, if the truth be told, I get a great deal of pleasure out of ridding the world of the dregs we feed on. The cities are a lot safer for the populace thanks to you and me."

Ernest smiled and put his cheek against Bookey's. "Let's go," he said. "It's party time." Bookey thought that was a funny expression coming from a three hundred year old man and he broke out laughing. They were both still laughing when they reached the lobby.

Larry was in the lobby reading a text book on the mathematics of nuclear power. "Whatever the fuck that is!" Bookey thought. Neither Bookey nor Ernest knew why, but they both knew that they wanted to help this boy.

"How much more money do you need to finish university?" Ernest asked Larry.

"Well, I owe two thousand in loans and I need about twelve thousand more to finish up. That's for tuition, books, supplies and just about everything else," Larry answered.

Ernest turned to Bookey. "Entertain the lad and don't let him get away. I'll be right back." Larry was flabbergasted when he saw Ernest leave the hotel lobby. He left so quickly, he was a blur. Bookey began to ask Larry about his ambitions in life. Larry wanted to be a nuclear physicist, and for the first time Booker thought about what he had given up. But he didn't have any regrets. His life was more fulfilled than he could ever imagine it would be. Before he could reflect further, Ernest was back. He was carrying a cloth sack which looked quite full.

He handed the sack to Larry and said, "There's twenty thousand dollars in this sack. Tell your boss to go fuck himself and take this home. Hide it in a safe place and tomorrow morning take it to the bank and put it into an interest bearing account. For tonight, when you get home change into something sexy and meet us at a gay bar called Blazing Saddles. We're meeting some friends there, and we want you to join us. I want to caution you about one thing. Be wise in any relationship you enter into. Don't let anyone tell you he loves you and needs to borrow money from you. If that happens run a country mile. A true lover will give, and not take, even when he has nothing material to give you."

Bookey wondered where the money had come from. He knew you couldn't get that much so quickly from an ATM machine. Finally he decided that what he didn't know would not harm him.

Larry stood there with his mouth open and his head nodding up and down. He was too shocked to react so Bookey slapped him on his butt and said, "Go, hurry, and we'll see you later." Larry shook his head as if to clear his thoughts and took off like a bat out of hell. On his way through the lobby he yelled at the front desk, to no one in particular, "I quit!!!"

"We just did a good deed for Larry and for humanity," Ernest said to Bookey. "Instinctively I know that someday he will be a great scientist and his work will benefit all mankind."

"Yes," Bookey said. "I feel the same way."

They found their way to Blazing Saddles and located their friends at the bar. The friends wanted to buy them drinks so they let them buy cokes, which they pretended to drink, and which they nursed all night. Bookey wondered what a coke would taste like now that he was no longer human, and he was tempted to take a sip. Ernest read his mind and shook his head to stop him. He whispered in Bookey's ear, "It will make you sick."

Blazing Saddles was a country western bar. Neither Bookey nor Ernest was familiar with line dancing steps, but they mastered it after just a few seconds of watching, and soon joined in the fun. They were there less than a half hour when Larry walked in. Wow, what a surprise. He was so hot in his shorts and sleeveless tee shirt. They introduced Larry to Maury and Terry, who were good friends, but not a couple. It was obvious immediately that Larry and Terry were attracted to each other. Ernest did a quick mind study of Terry and liked what he learned. He was a student at the University of

Toronto, just like Larry. They were both juniors. Terry's family was well off and he didn't have to work to pay his way through college. He was majoring in physical education. He looked like a phys-ed major, tall and muscular. Ernest smiled when he read Terry's soul and knew immediately that he was one of the good guys who would never harm anyone. Terry and Larry were made for each other. He looked up to see Bookey smiling and they nodded at each other.

During the evening, both Ernest and Bookey had a chance to chat one on one with both Terry and Larry. As they gazed into their human eyes, each of them suggested hypnotically that they would find a great love in the other. Larry and Terry were getting a double dose of hypnotic suggestion. By the end of the night, they couldn't stop kissing each other. When everyone else was gyrating to the music, those two were slow dancing, rubbing together and practically making love on the dance floor. "Our work is done," Ernest whispered to Bookey.

Terry and Larry couldn't wait to get out of the place, and seal their new found love. They said goodbye to Bookey and Ernest and kissed them on the cheek. They were both surprised that Bookey and Ernest felt so cold. It was very warm in the bar. Larry began to cry. "How can I thank you and where can I reach you?' he asked.

Ernest answered, "We don't stay very long in one place, but rest assured we will keep tabs on you, and we will contact you the next time we are in Toronto. Now go with Terry and both of you have a great life together."

As they left the bar, Larry and Terry assumed that these two were billionaires travelling the world and doing good deeds. Larry thanked God for his good fortune in meeting them.

Ernest and Bookey looked around to say goodnight and goodbye to Maury. They spotted him smooching with an older man of about forty. Forty or not, he was smashingly good looking. Maury was going to score, so they just left without saying goodbye.

They walked back to the hotel holding hands. "Where would you like to go next?" Ernest asked Bookey.

"I've given it a lot of thought and I'd like to visit your Italy," Bookey answered.

"I haven't wanted to go back there in all this time, but now I can't wait to go with you at my side."

"But we have no tickets or passports," Bookey reminded him.

Ernest just smiled. "They have internet service back at the hotel. I'll take care of everything," he said.

Ernest booked a flight leaving the next evening and arriving in Rome the following morning. He charged it to a real debit card which was his. He also booked it under his real name, Ernesto DiGrenato, the name on his credit card, and he booked Bookey under the name of John Smith. He figured that they might be looking for Bookey at Canadian airports by now.

"So that's how you got money from the ATM machine," Bookey said. "You have a real bank account and a real debit card."

"Of course, I do, little boy. What do you think I have been doing for three hundred years? I'm, I mean, we are very rich."

That got to Bookey and he needed to change the subject. "How will we manage arriving in the morning on probably a sunny day, and how will we manage without valid passports?" Bookey asked naively.

"I'll hypnotize the immigration agent who will think he has examined our passports. As for arriving in daylight, we'll just stay in the terminal away from windows until late afternoon."

"It can be kind of neat being supernatural," Bookey said. Ernest started to laugh and embraced his lover and student in a bear hug. He had to keep reminding himself that Bookey was still only a boy.

"Wow," Bookey said. "In about forty-eight hours we'll be in Rome. I can hardly process all this. How far is your home town from Rome?" he asked.

"I would guess it's about an hour's drive by today's technology. It used to be a day's coach ride when I lived there," Ernest answered.

"I can't wait to see it."

Chapter Three

The jumbo jet hit the tarmac screeching and belching as the reverse thrusters slowed the plane until it stopped completely. The Rome sun had just risen and was beating down on the airport. In the first class cabin two passengers donned sun glasses and lowered the window shades in their aisle. It seemed forever for the jet way to connect to the plane so they could disembark. They each had a small suitcase which had fit perfectly in the overhead compartment. It was all they had brought with them to Italy. They removed the luggage, and the taller man, the blond, left a book he had been reading on his seat. It was an Italian/English dictionary. He had mastered the Italian language during the flight. He spoke it in the modern vernacular, better than his companion Ernest did. They headed straight to customs and immigration.

They approached the immigration officer as a couple. He opened his mouth to ask the usual questions: Where were you born? What is the purpose of your visit? How long will you be staying? Etc. But he looked into Ernest's eyes and said not a word. He took his stamp instead, and stamped two invisible passports.

The custom's officer was no more inquisitive, and waived them right through. They entered the main terminal of the airport and looked around. There were plenty of shops, boutiques and watering holes for them to spend time in while waiting for the sun to go down. Ernest found an ATM machine and said to Bookey, "Come with me."

At the ATM machine he pulled out his debit card from his wallet, and said to Bookey, "By the time we get to the hotel tonight, there will be a duplicate card at the front desk in your name, Gianni Marioso. That was my lover's name and since we don't dare use your real name, I thought we would honor his memory by renaming you."

Gianni threw his arms around Ernesto. "I am so humbled," he said. He held back tears because he knew he would shed blood.

"I just wanted to show my love for you," Ernesto said. "My pin number is 1702, the year of my immortal birth. I have assigned you a pin number of 2011, the year of your immortal birth." Gianni was speechless.

Ernesto inserted his card and withdrew one thousand Euros from the machine. That was the maximum that was allowed. "We'll get more at the hotel tomorrow," he said.

They spent the day window shopping and snoozing in the terminal's waiting room. Sometime during the day, they each purchased (appropriated) clothing which they believed would make them look like residents and not tourists. Finally, Gianni nudged Ernesto, who had dozed off, and informed him that it was almost dark. They left the terminal and took a waiting cab to their hotel, which Ernesto had pre-booked in Toronto. The front desk clerk gave them an envelope when they checked in. It was Gianni's debit card, which he placed carefully in his wallet. Previously, he made sure that his wallet contained no remnants of his former life. He even reluctantly destroyed pictures of his parents. Silently, he wished them a good life.

Shortly after they settled into their hotel room, they showered and put on the clothing that they had gotten in the airport. They wore identical silk shirts, very narrow cotton trousers, socks and narrowing tapered leather shoes. Neither wore underwear and both looked very Italian, except for Gianni's Nordic looks.

Standing in front of the hotel, the teacher asked his student if he would like to find their quarry for this evening. Gianni smiled. "Thank you for your faith in me Ernesto." He sniffed the air and looked up the street. At the corner there stood two prostitutes plying their trade. "Come!" Gianni said.

Before they reached the ladies of the night, Gianni said, "The red head on the right is a single mother. Her husband deserted her and she is doing this to support her infant son. The brunette on the left does this because she is a whore and loves cock. Would you mind sharing tonight Ernesto? If we are still hungry we will find another."

I share my existence with you, love. I will share my dinner. Ernesto approached the red head and gave her some money. "Take the night off, my lovely," he said, "and spend some time with your son." She took the money, thanked her benefactor and ran off.

"How about me?" the other whore asked.

"We are both married and have no place to go. Do you have someplace to take us? We would both like to share your delights," Gianni said in perfect Italian.

The woman smiled coyly and said, "I can't be giving two pleasures for the price of one. You will both have to pay, and in advance." She named her price, and accepted imaginary money from Ernesto. She slipped the phantom Euros into her bra. "Follow me," she said, "it's only a short distance. She led them to a run down building and up a flight of stairs to a studio apartment. The bed she beckoned them to was filthy, and smelled of semen, urine and feces. Ernesto and Gianni were appalled. "Let's make short work of her," Gianni telepathically said to Ernesto, who nodded in total agreement.

The woman stripped in seconds. She put the imaginary Euros in a dresser drawer, and lay on the bed seductively. Her clients lay down with her fully clothed. She was about to ask why they didn't undress when one of them kissed her on the neck. With that kiss she felt sexual desire that she had not felt in years. Tiny little pin pricks made her shiver and she felt that she was swooning. Then she felt the other gentlemen kissing her neck on the other side. The pin pricks made her shiver all over and she felt an orgasm coming on. Before she could think about it, or be amazed, she passed out as her orgasm overcame her.

When they were done with her, Gianni asked "Did you have enough, my darling?"

"I'm satisfied for now, Gianni, but we'll have to feed again tomorrow. Hopefully, we can find two victims tomorrow to satisfy us for several days."

The lovers slit the woman's neck in order to disguise their teeth marks. They left the room and closed the door behind them.

We didn't get much sleep today," Ernesto observed. "I think I'd like to go back to the hotel, make love to you and sleep through the day tomorrow."

"You'll find me your willing slave," Gianni agreed smiling. Without caring who might see them in this derelict neighborhood, Gianni reached over and kissed Ernesto.

"Faggots," someone yelled, and suddenly a teen aged boy was coming at them with a baseball bat. Instinctively, Gianni, the athlete, stopped the boy's advance by grabbing his arm. Gianni had forgotten his new strength and the boy's arm ripped right off. Before he could scream out in pain, Ernesto clamped his hand over the boy's mouth.

"Feed," he hissed at Gianni. Gianni picked up the arm and drank it dry while Ernesto drank from the wound in the boy's torso.

Ernesto pulled away from the stricken boy. "He's still alive. Drink," he said to Gianni, who finished drinking what he could before the boy died.

"I'm strangely not hungry now," Ernesto said laughing.

"Neither am I," Gianni echoed. "Let's get out of here."

Their sexual desires were at a peak after such feasting, and they hurried back to the hotel. They put the "Do Not Disturb" sign on the door and double locked it. With the speed of lightening, they were naked in bed together, taking little nips from all over their bodies. They were intoxicated by the taste of their blood.

"Fuck me," Gianni yelled suddenly. "I need you inside of me so badly." Ernesto turned Gianni on his back and raised his legs. He positioned his cockhead at Gianni's abyss of desire. They never needed lubricant. Their ass holes were always slick with blood, especially after feeding. Ernesto slipped in easily and began stroking slowly, trying to prolong his orgasm, but to no avail. The second he came, and his blood began to spurt into Gianni, Gianni came with an unworldly scream.

They lay still for a while, kissing each other and pricking their tongues gently. Finally, satisfied for the moment, they showered away all the tell tale blood, wrapped up in each other's arms and slept for two days.

Two evenings later, they dressed and went down to the hotel lobby. They asked the concierge if he had a map of the greater Rome area. He said that he did and let them borrow it. Ernesto spread the map out on the concierge's desk and said to Gianni, "Look, here's my town. It used to be miles from Rome, but now it's right on the outskirts, a suburb, if you will."

They discussed taking a cab, but decided they could get there faster under their own foot power. They soared through the city so fast that they were a mere blur and went unseen by anyone.

When they arrived in the village, Ernesto was stunned. The eighteenth century hamlet was a bustling twenty-first century bedroom community. It was still early and residents were getting off buses they had boarded in Rome. Each of them hustled to waiting cars to be driven home by family members. Ernesto smiled at the changes. They were not for the better as far as he was concerned.

He stood there at the bus terminal with his head bowed and his eyes shut. Finally he said to Gianni, "Come this way." Gianni followed him and soon they were in an older section of town.

"There it is," Ernesto said. "It still stands." A very old church stood just ahead of them. "It's much smaller than I remember it." He advanced toward the church and started to enter.

"Is it safe for us to go in?" Gianni asked. Ernesto got hysterical with laughter.

"You've seen too many movies," he said.

When they entered the church, Ernesto instinctively dipped his fingers into the holy water and crossed himself. Gianni simply bowed his head.

"You're right," Gianni said. "I have seen too many movies. The holy water didn't sear your skin and kill you off." Now it was his turn to laugh.

A voice suddenly said to them, Is there something I can do for you, gentlemen?" They turned to see a very young and a very handsome priest standing behind them. He was very tall, about the same height as Gianni.

"No Father," Ernesto said. "We are Canadians, but I used to live here when I was very young and I attended this very church. In fact I was an altar boy."

The priest broke out into a big smile. He extended his arm and said, "Welcome, then! Welcome! I am Father James."

Ernesto and Gianni shook his hand and introduced themselves.

"My, you are both so cold. Can I offer you a cup of tea?" the priest asked.

"No thank you, Father. We can only stay a moment. I just wanted to see if the church had changed any. Are your quarters still behind the sanctuary?"

James looked confused. "No," he said, "I live in the parish house behind the church. The room behind the church is a social hall. It has been a social hall for at least fifty years, long before you were born."

"I guess I don't remember things as well as I thought I did," Ernesto smiled at the priest.

"Ernesto, we have to go now," Gianni said. He was afraid that Ernesto might say something he shouldn't.

Again they each shook the priest's hand, but this time they hypnotized him so that he felt a warm glow coming from the two men.

They stood outside the church for a few moments and out of habit Ernesto instinctively sniffed the air.

"What are you doing, love?" Gianni asked him.

Ernesto started to laugh. "Before you came to me, I constantly sniffed the air searching for another of my kind. I never had success."

"Teach me how." Gianni pleaded.

"It's simple. Smell me. Think how your mother smelled, how your father smelled. Can you sense the difference?"

"Yes, yes," Gianni said. He was excited. "I can smell your blood."

"That's it," Ernesto said. He was pleased with his student.

Suddenly Ernesto stopped smiling. He sniffed the air again several times. As white as his skin was, it surely turned whiter. "I smell another of our kind," he said, "and he is very close."

Gianni sniffed the air. "Yes," he said. "I smell him too. It seems to be coming from down that street." He pointed toward a passageway which was more like an alley than a street. He took Ernesto's hand and they started toward the alley. They walked cautiously down the narrow lane.

"The smell is stronger now," Ernesto said. A little bit later he stopped in front of a doorway. The name plate under the doorbell read, Francis Vinisti.

"I know that name, but it could not be him. He was my beloved teacher. What should we do?" he actually asked Gianni in confusion.

Gianni sensed Ernesto's distress and put his arms around him. "I suggest we ring the bell. We know that one of our kind lives here."

Ernesto nodded and moved his finger toward the bell. He was a good half inch away when the bell rang of its own volition. They heard a voice telepathically tell them to enter. "I know it is you, Ernesto, with a friend. I have waited for this day for three hundred years." The telepathic message said.

The door opened and after they entered, it closed behind them. Standing before them was a jolly looking, exceptionally handsome man with smiling eyes. He looked no more than thirty years old, but he was quite bald. He stood 5'9" tall and was short compared to Ernesto and Gianni. Gianni could smell the man's blood. It was a very pleasant odor, but much stronger than Ernesto's. He knew instinctively that Francis was much older than his lover.

Ernesto and Francis fell into each other's arms. Tears of blood flowed down both their cheeks. They began to wipe their blood with each other's tongues. Gianni began to feel hunger pangs.

"Sit! Sit!" Francis said beckoning them to a sofa. Ernesto offered what tears remained on his cheek to Gianni, who sucked them up greedily.

"Here, take mine too," Francis said to Gianni offering him his blood. Then he looked at Ernesto. "You must love him very much," he said. "You named him after Gianni." He had read their minds.

When they were all settled down and their tears were gone, Ernesto said to Francis, "I had no idea."

"Of course not," the kindly man said. "I loved my students too much to harm them. I am still a school teacher, but you should see the modern school I teach in and the tools I have at my hand. I can teach during the day as long as I keep out of the sun and keep the shades drawn in the classroom. Furthermore, I have been around a long time. I teach history from memory."

He broke out laughing at his own joke, and Gianni and Ernesto smiled politely.

"So that's why your classroom was always so dark," Ernesto commented. We always had to learn by the light of our lanterns."

"Well, we use electric lights now," Francis said.

"Let me tell you my story," he said, and his two guests listened intently.

"I was born in Pompeii in ancient times. I fell in love with a young man when I was nearing thirty. I knew that he loved me too, but he kept avoiding having sex with me. One day he said that he could resist no longer and he took me to bed. I drank his blood when he came in my mouth, and he agreed to turn me so we could be together forever." Ernesto took Gianni's hand and they smiled at each other. Francis continued.

"We were lovers for almost ten years. I was a merchant of perfumes in those days, and business took me to Rome. While I was there, Mt. Vesuvius erupted. My lover was killed by one of the few things that can kill us, fire. He was burned to a crisp, and I was devastated. For the next fifty or so years I slept as much as I could, hoping to forget my sorrow. Finally, I knew I had to get back into the world. I vowed to use my power for good. I settled in this small town and decided to be a teacher of young children. There is no greater calling. At night I would speed into Rome where I could find any number of derelicts to feed on. I clouded the minds of the residents here so that nobody realized that I never aged. I was able to continue my profession for centuries." He stopped to take a breath, and he smiled at his two companions. He was so full of joy, that he could barely continue his story.

"I had trained myself over the years to stop feeding a second or two before my prey died. That way I never had to spit out bitter blood. This practice led to my one terrible mistake.

"Your parish priest, Ernesto, was old and deformed. He made a habit of drugging young men and having sex with them in his quarters. I determined to feed on him and make the town safer for its young men. I entered his quarters one evening. Of course, he did not resist me. I drank of his blood, but I stopped before he died. Somehow, I must have stopped too soon, and he survived. Unfortunately he had turned in the process.

"The next Sunday, there he was in church. You actually sat next to me, Ernesto, and I put my arm around you. You were mourning the death of your lover, Gianni. When I put my arm around you, I could smell that you were newly turned. I read your mind, and I vowed revenge, but a few nights later, you did it for me. To my sorrow, you disappeared too. In a sense, Ernesto, you are my grandson and Gianni is my great grandson." Once again he laughed at his own joke.

Gianni and Ernesto stood up and embraced Francis. The teacher looked at them and said, "Please stay the night with me and sleep here tomorrow during the day. You can't imagine how lonely I have been. The children keep me going, but it's not enough. I beg you to exchange blood with me."

Gianni wasn't sure, but his recent mortal self was telling him that Francis was asking them for a three way. His immortal self-told him that if he exchanged blood with someone so ancient, he would become an even stronger immortal. Ernesto and Francis read his mind and nodded at him. He nodded back and Francis began to disrobe.

They made love for hours. Each of them came repeatedly and each had a chance to be in the middle. Gianni was first in that position. When Francis's blood spewed down his throat and Ernesto's blood shot up his intestines, he experienced an orgasm that he could never be able to describe. The only thing he knew for sure was that no human orgasm had ever come close, and this immortal orgasm surpassed all others to date.

Francis kept crying over and over. "Thank you, thank you. I know that you must go, but I wish you could stay forever."

Ernesto told him, that they would surely return one day, but for now his mission was to show the world to his newly turned student. The next morning, Francis went to work with a spring in his step and a look of great satisfaction on his face. When he came home the sun was low enough in the sky for his guests to leave. They waited for dark, however, so that their return to Rome could go unnoticed.

Chapter Four

For twenty years Ernesto and Gianni circumnavigated the globe. Except for Francis they did not run into another of their kind, although they really tried hard to find someone. During that time they visited every exotic port of call that Gianni, or Booker, had ever read about.

Finally one night in Cairo, Gianni said to Ernesto, "My love, I am getting tired of all this travel. I'd like to stay put in one place for a while, if that's alright with you."

"Anything you want," Ernesto answered. "I was just waiting for you to tell me when you were ready to rest from travelling. Is there any particular place you would like to settle?"

"I'm an American and would prefer to settle in The States, but not the west coast. At least, not until everyone I once knew is dead. How about New York? It's an exciting city and we would have plenty of appropriate persons to feed on."

Ernesto didn't answer so Gianni said, "I'm sorry, my darling. I am being so selfish. Perhaps you would prefer to live in Rome?"

"No, not at all," Ernesto answered. In fact I was just reminiscing about my days in the States. That's where I met you, and I have a special affinity to everything that is you." Gianni kissed Ernesto and off they went to feed.

They flew from Cairo to Rome and spent a few days there with Francis. Since all flights from Rome to New York left in early morning, Ernesto, Gianni and Francis went to the airport the night before. Francis insisted on seeing them off. The three immortals spent the night in the terminal and then Francis intended to spend the day there before leaving for home.

Alone in the airport after the flight left for New York, a young man approached Francis. He was a male prostitute and said that he charged only 100 Euros. "Where can we go?" Francis asked innocently.

"I'm just a short car ride from the airport," the young man informed him.

"That's fine. Let's go." Francis said. He put on his dark glasses and pulled his baseball cap low over his face. He left his auto at the airport, and he hailed a cab. The driver started off, following the young man's directions.

"What would you like to do?" the young prostitute asked.

"Suck your cock, of course," Francis answered. Just as he spoke these words, the cab stopped in front of an apartment building. They were in a very nice, middle class neighborhood. Francis paid the cab fare, and the man took Francis to a second floor one bedroom apartment. It was neat and smelled clean. For a moment Francis had second thoughts about this particular prostitute, but when he smelled his blood, all reason left him.

They undressed quickly, and the man said to Francis, "You have a beautiful body. It will be a pleasure to make love with you. Some of my clients are so grotesque I have trouble getting hard." Having said that, he waved his very hard cock at Francis, who immediately fell to his knees and swallowed the man's enormous cock right down to his pubic hair.

He sucked the cock for some time just for the pleasure of it, but the engorged member was pulsating with blood and his resistance was weakening. Finally he bit into it, and started to suck out all the blood. The man felt no pain, only pleasure, as he swooned and passed into oblivion.

New York was the perfect place for Gianni and Ernesto. They were in the city that never sleeps. There were hundreds of mortals who lived in the city mostly at night, so they had plenty of company, especially in the gay bars.

They were never at a loss for prey. Every alley produced a predator ready to slit their throats and empty their wallets.

They bought an apartment in Trump Towers, and called themselves Ernest and Johnny. They tipped generously and everybody liked them. They settled into a life of theater and museum going. They contributed heavily to charities supporting the arts, but never neglected charities that helped abused and battered women and children; charities which did medical research and those which provided education for poor students who would otherwise be left without an education. They were welcomed into New York's high society as well as New York's gay community.

They loved their existence, but they knew that they would have to make a change before everyone noticed that they were not aging. They were in their twelfth year in New York, when they sold their apartment and announced that they were moving to San Francisco. They chose this city because it was in Johnny's home state but still far from his former home. He had been gone from Los Angeles for thirty-two years. They had made a decision to live in San Francisco for fifteen years, and then, if they wanted to, it would be safe to move back to Los Angeles. Ernest was still paying rent on his very humble apartment so he knew it was still in existence.

In San Francisco they kept a much lower profile than they had in New York. They were party goers and hopped from one gay bar to another so that they were never pegged as regulars at any of them. They made many friends and had to cloud their minds into thinking that they were aging along with them.

One day they were delighted to read in the paper a story about Larry Simpson (the young student they had helped in Toronto.) He had developed a new rocket engine which would make space travel so easy and so cheap that it was predicted that space travel for the average person would be no more costly than the average airline ticket in the very near future. There was a picture of him and his spouse (he and Terry got married in Toronto where it was legal) alongside the article. They were about sixty now, but looking just as handsome as when they were young.

When it was time to leave San Francisco and head back to Los Angeles, they made a decision not to make close mortal friends like they had done in other cities. That way they could stay there longer. They also decided to leave the small cell Ernest had been renting all these years, and get a more suitable apartment. They rarely took prey home and didn't need a home which was virtually a hiding place. Consequently, they purchased a three bedroom condominium with a large terrace looking out over the whole city.

As soon as they got settled in LA, they drove to the cemetery where Johnny knew his parents would be buried. He was pleased to read on their tombstones that they had both enjoyed long lives. On the way home, they drove by his old house. What a shock! The entire street was filled with high rise luxury condominiums. Johnny was saddened that all the old stately homes that had stood on a tree lined street were now gone. Reading his mind, Ernest said, "Dearest, after all these years, you are still not used to accepting the changes of time. You'll get used to it, I promise you."

"As long as our love remains constant, I don't care what changes around us," Johnny answered.

During all the years that they had been together, they visited Rome at the end of every school year and Francis visited them before the new school year was to begin. Johnny and Ernest were waiting for Francis's plane to arrive at LAX one very warm August evening. They were very excited anticipating the exchange of blood that was to occur between them. As much as they loved each other, their orgasms were maximized by the amount of blood flowing between the three immortals, and especially by the blood of the ancient man. The three of them always slept in the same bed. Ernest had contracted for a custom bed which was a foot wider than a king size and he had linens custom made as well.

As usual Francis got off the plane with no luggage. They would go on a shopping spree as soon as possible. Unfortunately, he was unable to wear any of their clothes because they both towered over him.

Ernest drove home as quickly as he could. They disrobed and hit the oversized bed in mind boggling speed. They began their ritual of love with their guest in the middle. Johnny sucked Francis's cock while Ernest fucked him. As speedily as they had begun their love making, they slowed down to a sensuous pace trying to prolong the inevitable. They changed positions after each one had cum and had deposited his blood inside someone or on someone. No blood was wasted. They each shared the blood that was on one of their bodies. Hours later when it was all over, they fell asleep and slept through the next day. Shopping for Francis would have to wait until the following evening.

When they awoke the next evening, they showered together and then changed the linens which had no blood on them, but which smelled of blood. They had no need to feed but went shopping for clothes for Francis. They went to Rodeo Drive where everything was overpriced and where they paid for nothing. They went home where they all changed into clothes appropriate for bar hopping, and then they started out for West Hollywood, which remained a gay Mecca after all these many years.

They were sitting in a gay bar pretending to sip drinks, but actually enjoying the eye candy when Francis said, "I need to talk to you about something. I am prompted to share this with you because you have both told me many times how you dreamed about each other before you actually met. Well, I am having a similar experience." He stopped to gather his thoughts and to pretend to drink from his glass.

"Right after your visit early this summer," he went on as Ernest and Johnny listened intently, "I began to dream that I was in America at a gay bar. I saw a man there who was a few years older than the age I was when I was turned. I'd say he was about thirty-three to thirty-five. He was also about two inches taller than I; just under six feet. He was dark with close cropped curly hair. He looked Greek or Italian, Greek I think. He was very muscular and in my dream he didn't quite approach me, but rather we approached each other. We began to talk and he said his name was Martin. He was a personal trainer and he was very attracted to me. I went home with him and we made wild, passionate love. In my dream I emitted semen and my tears were real, and very salty. I could actually taste them. I was crying because he told me that he loved me and he wanted to be with me for all eternity. He was crying also and said that he would give up his life for me. He said that he would follow me back to Italy but would prefer if we lived here and tied our lives to Johnny and Ernest. Yes, my loves, he used your names. I told him I loved him too and wanted to be with him forever. I told him that I had not felt this way since I lost my first love centuries ago. He begged me not to leave him, and I promised that we would be together forever."

He stopped for a moment and since Johnny and Ernest were speechless, he continued. "I have had this identical dream every time I go to sleep and sometimes I have this dream more than once in one sleep cycle. The amazing thing is I remember every time I have the dream and every detail in it. I think I am going mad. I look for Martin everywhere I go, on the streets, in shops, in the airplane, and in every bar we have gone to, because in my dream, we meet in a bar."

"Wow," his friends said simultaneously.

"That's truly amazing," Johnny said. "I dreamed about Ernest for many years every time I whacked off. I could describe every detail of his body before we met."

"I only dreamed of Johnny once before we met, but he was as real to me as you two are, sitting with me right now," Ernest added.

The three immortals were so caught up in this conversation that even they failed to notice a good looking muscular man approaching their table. He was just under six feet tall with short, curly hair. His eyes were dark and his long eyelashes made them look very sensual. He was wearing jeans and a tee shirt with no sleeves, which accentuated his muscular body. He had tears in his eyes.

Finally the three men looked up when they heard a voice say, "Francis is that you? I'm Martin."

Ernest and Johnny were rarely surprised and they had little reason to ever gasp, but this time they did, especially when Martin said, "And you must be Johnny and Ernest. I have been dreaming about all of you all my life, and especially you, Francis, and about making love to you. You are exactly as I have seen you in my dreams."

Francis jumped up. He wanted to embrace Martin and kiss him, but he was afraid of the consequences. "Don't be afraid," Johnny sent him a message telepathically, so Francis grabbed Martin and began to kiss him.

"Your kisses are as sweet as in my dreams," Martin said, and Francis sighed with relief. Then Martin added, "Your body is as warm and inviting as I imagined it would be. Now that I have found you, I'm not letting you go. I have been looking for you all my adult life."

"And I have been seeking you all summer also, ever since I began to dream of you." Francis was forcing himself not to cry. He dare not let Martin see his blood tears, but Martin said in a trance like voice, "Cry, my love, just as I am crying. It won't matter at all. I know how tortured you are trying to hold back your tears."

Francis sat down in his chair and lowered his face as he began to cry. Martin sat down in the fourth chair at their table. He took Francis's head in his hands and began to kiss away his tears of blood. As he did that, his body began to radiate a glowing aura.

Suddenly Francis stopped him. "Not here, not now, not this way," he said. "Do you really want to be with me for eternity?" Martin smiled and nodded vigorously.

"Turn me," he said softly to Francis. I want to spend all eternity with you."

"Let's go to our place," Ernest said. "You guys can use the guest bedroom. When you have turned Martin, Francis, join us and we will all exchange blood. Francis you are the father of us all, and that will be an appropriate thing to do. The three immortals and the human embraced each other in a group hug. They got Ernest's car out of the parking lot and hurried to the condominium. Francis and Martin never stopped kissing and fondling each other in the back seat. When they got to the apartment, all four of them were tenting their trousers. Ernest ran to the kitchen and gave Francis a sharp knife.

Francis hurried Martin into the guest bedroom. It was impossible to ignore the sounds of ecstatic love making coming from the room, and that got Ernest and Johnny going in their bedroom.

The first thing Francis did was to slit his wrist and ask Martin to drink as much of his blood as he could before his skin closed and healed. As much as Martin had enjoyed the taste of Francis's tears he drank the blood offered to him with fervor. It reacted on him like an aphrodisiac. Before the wrist was healed, Martin had an orgasm. He emitted semen but it was mixed with blood.

"Suck my cock," Francis said. His voice was somewhere between a plea and a teacher's instruction. Martin had been sucking cock for nearly twenty years, since he was fifteen, but never had any cock tasted so good to him. He felt like he was devouring a mixture of honey and whipped cream. He was good at what he was doing and Francis came quickly, gushing blood down Martin's waiting gullet, and screaming in ecstasy.

Immortals don't need a recovery period. They need only smell blood to react sexually. "Let me fuck you now," Francis said, and send my blood up into your belly."

"Please, please! I have waited forever for this" was all Martin could say. Francis was well lubricated with his blood and Martin's saliva so he entered Martin easily. He had not fucked anybody he loved this much since his days in Pompeii, and he came in even more ecstasy than before. His blood spurted up and travelled through Martin's intestines. Martin's skin was glowing and Francis was sure he had turned. He determined to find out. He rolled Martin onto his back and went down on him. Martin was so pumped up he came quickly. Pure blood spurted down Francis's throat.

"You are immortal now, my love."

They lay wrapped up in each other's arms for a while and Francis said to his eternal partner, "Come now, my love, and we will give you even greater pleasure. They entered the master bedroom and found Ernest and Johnny playing sixty-nine. They stopped playing when Martin and Francis entered the room. They jumped out of bed and embraced Martin.

"Welcome to our world," Ernest said. "We want you both to know that we look forward to spending eternity with the two of you. As much as we love each other it's really nice to have the company of others of our kind with whom we can exchange our blood. Come friends, join us in bed."

They all climbed into the oversized bed and formed a daisy chain. Ernest, Johnny and Francis knew what to expect, but Martin was unprepared for the orgasm he experienced. It brought him to tears, which his friends happily devoured. When Martin composed himself, they took turns fucking each other until each of them had fucked every one of the others. Each time Martin came (and he marveled that he could have so many orgasms), the intensity of his orgasms increased. When someone's blood shot up his ass, he would have another orgasm of ecstatic intensity. He had no idea what forces had brought him to Francis, but in his mind he thanked those forces over and over. Francis did the same. The four of them finally fell asleep in the big oversized bed and slept for three days.

The next few weeks were busy ones for the four immortals. Besides helping Martin to adapt to his new status, like teaching him how to feed, and how to protect himself from the sun, if he had to go out during the day, they had a lot of business to take care of. It was a whirlwind of activity for all of them since they acted as a family unit.

The first thing they did was to go to a nearby Wells Fargo bank and arrange for all of Francis's assets to be transferred to America. When the bank manager saw the sum of money that was coming to his branch, he nearly fainted. The money was transferred in both Francis's and Martin's names. Immediately, two financial advisors descended on Francis, who couldn't care less. He signed some papers for them and gave them carte blanche to invest his money. He told them only one thing. If you don't increase my net worth by 5% within a year, I'll hire someone else. Five percent, indeed! That came to roughly a million and a half dollars.

Francis called his school principal and told him that he would not be returning. Then he called a mortal friend who had the keys to his apartment. He asked him to tell the landlord that he was not coming back, but he would send him three month's rent. He told the friend to take what he wanted from the apartment and give the rest to charity.

There was a condominium for sale just two doors down the hall from Ernest and Johnny. It was exactly the same as theirs, and Francis purchased it, again in joint names. Martin objected stating that he couldn't afford it and they all laughed and assured him that he could. They paid cash and since the condominium was empty, they moved right in.

The four of them went to Martin's apartment where he was on a month to month lease. He gave one month's notice to the manager but told him that the apartment would be available in one week if he could rent it that soon. Martin had very good taste and he had some beautiful furniture including some expensive antiques. They arranged to have almost all of it moved within forty-eight hours. What they didn't take, Martin gave to his favorite charities.

Since Martin only had a one bedroom apartment they went shopping for furniture for the other two bedrooms. Martin had only a small dinette so they also purchased a formal dining room set and outdoor furniture for the terrace.

Lastly, Martin had to take care of personal business. His parents were dead and he had no living relatives that he knew of, so there was nobody to inform of his whereabouts, wherever that might be. At the urging of his new immortal family, he quit his job. He told his co-workers that he had been adopted by a sugar daddy and would be travelling the planet. He only had one close friend who was straight. The friend was married and had a family. Martin gave him his new address and told him that he was moving in with a new lover and would stay in touch, but of course that didn't happen. Within a week of his transition, the mortal Martin Masarius ceased to exist, and the immortal Martin Mason took his place. In modern Italy, Francis had taken the name of Francis Vinisti, and for at least the next hundred years, Frances Vinisti and Martin Mason lived together in this building until it was condemned, and they and their closest friends were forced to move.

The first weeks of Martin's transformation were fun weeks for all of them. They were caught up in teaching Martin to handle his immortality, in shopping for and decorating a new apartment, and in buying Martin new clothing, which he would not have splurged on before.

They hardly ever left their condominium complex. They would sleep all day. In the evening they would go out and feed and then play cards and board games all night, but they all jokingly agreed to honor a pact not to read each other's minds while they were playing. They particularly enjoyed strip poker. Fortunately or unfortunately, as the case may be, this game usually terminated in wild and bloody sex.

As for sex, they participated mostly with their own partners, but once a month, when the moon was full, they exchanged blood together. By not doing that as a regular diet, they kept it very special and something to look forward to.

Sometimes they would go to the bar where Francis and Martin had met. They would pretend to sip a drink, but mostly they enjoyed the eye candy. Occasionally they spotted a suitable candidate for dinner and they followed him out of the bar to feed upon. But the main purpose of visiting the bar was just to sit and enjoy each other's company. For centuries, Ernest and Francis had lived a world apart in abject loneliness, and now they were part of a loving family. Every day they thanked the powers that be for their good fortune and for the loves in their lives.

During the course of these conversations, Francis, Ernest and Johnny
often reminisced about experiences they had had in foreign lands. Martin
listened but felt left out. He had never been outside of the United States.
He suppressed any feelings of envy so that it was difficult to read his
mind. Besides Martin, Johnny was the closest to having been human and
experiencing human thoughts. One day, he sensed Martin's desire to travel.

"You know what?" Johnny asked the group. "Why don't we make a travel
plan spread out over the next few years so that we can have the pleasure of
introducing Martin to all the strange, unique and exotic places in the world?"

They all nodded and thought it was a great idea. Johnny continued, "Let's
take two months every year and visit one continent a year. We'll start with
South America, travel the globe and end up back in North America where
we can do our own country, Mexico and Canada."

"Fantastic idea," Francis said. "What fun it will be to show Martin the
world."

"I know," Ernest agreed. "That's how I felt with Johnny.

"When we get to Canada, Ernest, let's visit Larry and Terry. We can cloud
their minds to think we are as old as they."

They began to make plans. They didn't have to rush like on that hectic
night that Ernest had experienced rushing Bookey out of the country. They
applied for and received legitimate passports. They bought sufficient
money orders to see them through two months, give or take a week, in South
America. They all learned to speak Spanish and Portuguese in a few hours,
and practiced by speaking it to each other. They poured over a map of the
continent and listed the cities they wanted to visit. Based on the length of
their stay and the size of the city, they allotted a certain number of days to
visit each place.

They began their trip in Caracas in Venezuela, at the northern end of South
America, and worked their way down and across the continent. In Caracas,
they rented a mid-size car. They were afraid a large car would not negotiate

some of the narrow highways and streets along the way. They had very little luggage to concern themselves about.

Each city in each country left a memory for each of them, but they spent a full two weeks in Rio. They encountered only one problem in their entire sojourn in South America. They were in agreement that the old adage was correct: Latin men are hot, hot, hot! They desired so many of them, that they were constantly stressed about harming a good soul. It was a minor problem, however. The pimps and prostitutes soon made themselves known to the four handsome strangers, especially to the two younger looking ones. Youth is desired everywhere in the world.

They spent many happy evenings in gay bars throughout the continent. Some were out in the open and others were like the speakeasies of the prohibition days in the United States. They pretended to drink and enjoyed the company of a cross section of gay men in every country. They fitted in easily with raw youths and senior citizens.

They were particularly fond of feeding on pimps. Too many of the male prostitutes had little choice in their less than chosen profession. Extreme poverty, coupled with extreme good looks, opened many doors for them in the sex industry and helped put them on a sound financial footing. But the pimps treated their boys like slaves. They gave them a very small cut of the evening's take. To add insult to injury, at the end of the day, many of the pimps raped their prostitutes.

It was always a pleasure to tell the pimp that they desired him over any of the prostitutes. The pimp saw it as a way to keep the whole fee, and the fee for a foursome was especially high. Sometimes they read the mind of a prostitute and discovered that he would often beat his customer senseless and steal his wallet. When that happened the foursome would say that they wanted both the pimp and the prostitute because they didn't think one man could satisfy all four of them. The hired twosome was delighted. They had weapons which they believed could easily overwhelm these fops, and that would give them four wallets to plunder.

Feeding on scum like these low lives was always a special delight to the immortals, and often, as a reward to themselves after the meal, the four would exchange their own blood with each other as if it was dessert.

But the best part of travelling, as everyone knows, is coming home. The trips they made over the years were just long enough to satisfy them and short enough so that they didn't get tired of it. Once back in Los Angeles, they resumed their 'normal' existence, and made jokes about foreign meals.

After they had visited all the continents, they avoided boredom by opening businesses. They ran a string of gay bars over the years catering to different segments of the gay community. These establishments did not open until late afternoon so that the proprietors could always be present.

The difficult part of being immortal was watching good friends age and die. As hard as it was for all of them, they always got through it and found solace in each other.

They would console each other by exchanging blood and wondering if there was really such a thing as eternity. Ever on their minds was the thought that their eternity might have a finite ending. It wasn't a dreadful thought. In fact they looked forward to the day.

MURDER ON THE HUDSON

Chapter One

I entered the lobby of my apartment building, and did what I always do upon arriving home from work. I opened my mailbox and retrieved the current day's collection of bills and junk mail. Today's mail was a little different than on other days. Among the usual stuff, one envelope stood out. It was square and at least six inches by six inches. Whoever had addressed it had used a calligrapher. The lettering was ornate, in black ink, which stood out on the very pale lavender envelope. There was no return address on the envelope.

I let myself into my fourth floor apartment and did what I do every day. I threw the mail on the hall table. I undressed to my birthday suit and put all my dirty clothes in the hamper in the laundry room. I took a long, therapeutic shower, and cleansed my body as well as I possibly could, paying particular attention to my cock, balls and ass hole. It's important for me to do this every evening. It's imperative that I wash the scum of the earth out of my hair and off my body.

I'm a police detective you see. Every day I associate with the dregs of New York City society. I have to touch them, sometimes handcuff them, and even undress them to look for hidden weapons. You have no idea how my skin cringes when I have to perform these duties. I feel filthy. Not only do I feel contamination all over my body, but I feel the slime invading my soul as well. My evening shower is my salvation.

How different is my morning shower. In the morning I cleanse myself of the evidence of love from the night before. I carefully wash the dried semen out of my trimmed pubic hairs and my belly button. I give equal attention to the remaining semen which might still be residing in my ass hole. As I wash, I remember the evening before.

After my evening shower, I make myself a light dinner. If I don't wish to bother, I'll have some fast food at Burger King or McDonalds. That shit is all the same to me. Then I go to my favorite gay bar, Dudes on East 86th Street. All my friends hang out there. Dudes caters to an older crowd, usually from the mid-thirties and older. Consequently one does not have to suffer deafness from loud disco music. By the third beer, no later, I am sure to be hit on. I'm not particular. As long as he's clean looking and clean smelling I'm always up for man sex.

We usually go to my place which is in the neighborhood, but sometimes I can sense mistrust, and my trick wants to go to his place. I feel my weapon hidden inside the waist band of my trousers and I accompany him without fear. Up to this point in my life, my tricks have always been honest and I have not had to use my gun at all.

I am a very diversified lover, and this encourages most of my tricks to be the same way. It is rare for a trick to balk at doing anything I might ask for. I love to use fellatio as foreplay and fucking to achieve orgasm. I find that most men feel the same way. I give and I take. I never get a complaint. Why would I? I am well hung, seven inches, cut and thick. My tricks love to fondle me, and can't resist sucking me. I am always true to my promise to go slowly and gently, and to be well greased when I fuck them. It is rare that I don't have a sex partner for the evening, but when I don't, I use my fist. My fist is educated and lubed for maximum pleasure.

On this particular evening, I got out of the shower and dressed very casually in denim shorts, a tank top and sandals. I had already decided to do fast food this evening. Before going out I always open the mail. All bills are placed in a pile to be paid on the weekend. Junk mail is thrown in the circular file. Of course, this day, there was the lavender envelope to open.

I am very meticulous and did not wish to damage this particular invitation so I slit it open slowly with a letter opener. Like the envelope, the enclosed invitation was lavender as well, but the color was deeper, a light purple. I removed the invitation and read:

You are cordially invited to spend the
Labor Day Weekend, from Friday evening
To Monday evening,
At my home in Nyack, New York
201 River Street
(clothing optional)
Monte Barnes

Enclosed with the invitation was a stamped, return envelope for the RSVP. I was astounded. I had met Monte only once. He is a well-heeled Broadway producer. Most of his plays and musicals have been resounding successes.

One afternoon about four months earlier, I had been called upon to investigate a suspicious backstage accident at one of Monte's productions. The male lead had tripped over a prop placed carelessly where it should not have been. His right leg suffered multiple fractures, and his understudy was set to fill in that night. Most investigators would assume that the understudy was the prime suspect, but that is not my MO. Everybody in the theater was my suspect.

Sitting at a table backstage, I interviewed every member of the cast and crew. Monte chose to be present at the interviews, and to tell the truth that was all right with me. Monte is a gorgeous hunk of a man. All during the interviews he kept staring at my crotch, and I wondered if he might not be my trick for this evening.

I concluded my interviews about an hour before curtain time. I was certain that there had been no foul play and that a stage hand had left the prop there by accident. Everyone was relieved.

Monte graciously offered me an opportunity to see the show that night. It was a hit musical and seats were hard to get except for months in the future. I had intended going right home from there anyway, so I accepted.

"I'll send out for sandwiches," he said. "We can eat in my office and later we can watch the show from my box. Follow me!"

I followed him to his office. We sat and chatted, mostly about some of my more interesting cases. After the sandwiches and sodas were delivered, Monte locked his door. He came over to where I was sitting, leaned down and kissed me full on the lips. Naturally I offered no resistance.

"How about some action after the show?" he asked knowing full well what my answer would be. I am sure he could see the bulge in my pants.

"Sounds like a great plan to me," I answered

Sitting in his box in the darkened theater, we kept groping each other all through the show. Often we leaned toward each other and brushed our lips together. Monte was nice and hard and I could tell that he was at least as big as I am, but I guessed he was not as thick. That would be fine with me especially when he fucked me. He told me that he maintained an apartment in the city, but his real home was across the Hudson River in Nyack, NY. He asked if I would like to go to his apartment after the show. I gladly accepted.

Monte's apartment was lavishly furnished in a baroque style. Upon entering it, I felt like I was entering a brothel in the nineteenth century. It certainly started all my sex juices flowing. As best as I can remember, Monte and I had fantastic sex together that night. We started in his shower and continued throughout the night in his bed. I can only assume that was the reason he invited me for what promised to be a sex filled weekend at his primary residence in Nyack. I was pleased to note that my sexual prowess had made me memorable.

I had not taken any vacation in quite a while, and if I didn't take time off soon, I would lose some of my days. I quickly put in for time off over the Labor Day weekend. When it was granted, I sent Monte my RSVP. The Friday before Labor Day most of my co-workers left the office early and I was among them. I went home and had my evening shower early. I packed lightly remembering that clothing was optional. In addition, the weather reports for the weekend promised us scorching temperatures.

Nyack is a lovely, quaint town, northwest of Manhattan, on the other side of the Hudson River. You can drive there from midtown Manhattan in about forty-five minutes. It boasts many antique shops and stately old mansions. A good many theater people from New York own homes there. The most famous inhabitant ever was Helen Hayes. A hospital in the County bears her name as she was the chief endower. It is a very gay friendly, and gay inhabited, town and I have been there more than once enjoying the gourmet restaurants and frequent street fairs.

I drove west across the Tappan Zee Bridge. Nyack is situated just the other side of the bridge. The late afternoon sun in the western sky was blinding me, and I was happy to get off the bridge. With the help of my GPS system, I found River Street and wound my way up a hilly road to 201.

A handsome young man, wearing a Bikini bathing suit answered the door. The weekend was starting well. The young man was delightful eye candy. After I identified myself, he took my overnight bag, which mainly contained toiletries, and asked me to follow him. He carried my bag to a room that I knew immediately was the master bedroom. Obviously Monte had further designs on me, although at the moment, I preferred this young man.

"My name is Larry," he said. If you need anything at all during the weekend just let me know. We are expecting only one more guest. When he arrives, I'll take off my bathing suit. In the meantime, why don't you strip and go down to the pool. The other guests are already there."

"How many guests are there?" I asked.

"When the last guest arrives, we'll have eleven," he said, "but Mr. Barnes and I make thirteen."

Not that I am superstitious, but I didn't like that number at all. I stripped naked and hung my scant wardrobe in one of several walk in closets in the room. As I went downstairs to find the pool, I was struck by the stark contrast of this house to Monte's town house. It was so modern and so sparsely furnished that it was almost surreal. The walls were hung with abstract paintings in white and black. There was absolutely no color in the house. All the furniture was gray, black or white, with an occasional piece of silver.

Totally naked, I made my way down the stairs and out the back door. When I got to the pool area I was astonished. You should know that it takes a lot to astonish me. There were some of the most beautiful male bodies I had ever seen. Practically everyone was sporting an erection and some had coupled off and were enjoying oral and anal sex right out in front of everyone. Nobody in this crowd seemed in the least shy or inhibited.

Monte spotted me and ran over to greet me. He hugged me and pulled me tight against his naked body. His right hand cupped my balls and stroked my cock and instantly I was as hard as the rest of the crowd.

"I took the liberty of putting you in with me," he said. "I hope you don't mind."

"Not at all," I answered and kissed Monte full on his lips. We were interrupted by Larry, the houseboy. He was still wearing his bikini bathing suit so I assumed that the last guest had not yet arrived. He was carrying a tray of hors d'oevres and offered us some.

Monte pointed over his left shoulder and said, "The bar is over there. Help yourself and mix your own drinks." I had an hors d'oevres in my right hand so Monte took my left hand and led me over to meet the rest of the guests.

He introduced me to Barry, Elroy, Abel, Grant, Francis, Don, Conrad, Ian and Harry.

"You'll never remember all the names," Monte said, "so don't strain yourself." Monte was unaware of my police training. At that moment I could name every guest at the pool without hesitation. As an extra added attraction, I could even describe each cock in minute detail. Let me not forget, I could also describe every tattoo and body piercing, and to whom it belonged.

I had just finished shaking the last hand when the doorbell rang. Larry put down the tray of hors d'oevres and disappeared into the house. I figured that it would take Larry seven minutes to reappear without his Bikini, and the last guest would get to the pool in fifteen minutes after being shown to his room and given time to undress.

Larry reappeared in nine minutes carrying a fresh tray of pigs in a blanket. I hadn't counted on that, and I chided myself for not factoring in his household duties. He was now nude of course, and I could see immediately why Monte kept him around. As eye candy, he was looking better and better to my horny eyes.

The last guest appeared in exactly fifteen minutes. He was probably the oldest man present. He looked to be in his early fifties, but no matter. He was buff and muscular and sported a better than ample package and he was still flaccid. Monte introduced him around and came to me last.

"Ken, my dear friend," he said to me. "In case you were worried about us being raided. I'd like you to meet Jason. He's our chief of police here in Nyack." Then he turned to Jason. "Chief, I'd like you to meet Ken. He's a detective with the New York City Police Department. You two should have lots to talk about." I noticed that surnames were completely taboo.

Jason and I shook hands warmly. I asked him if he would like a drink because I was just on my way to the bar to make one for myself. He nodded and we headed that way together. By this time the sun was very low in the sky, and suddenly lights were turned on, illuminating the pool and the pool area. Jason mixed himself a scotch and soda and I made a vodka tonic. I motioned to two lounge chairs at poolside which were unoccupied and we claimed them for ourselves. We began to talk some shop and I couldn't help being envious of the quiet life of Nyack's police chief. Crimes were minimal and violent crimes almost non-existent.

In the middle of our conversation, Jason stood up and sat down on my lounge chair. I had to scoot over to make room for him. "You're hot," he said and he laid his hand across my package. He started to stroke my cock and then he started to lean over as if he was going to blow me. Out of nowhere, Monte appeared. He pushed Jason away from me.

"Not tonight, Chief. This one's mine," Monte said. I could swear his tone was menacing. Jason glared at Monte, and he jumped up and made his exit. Frankly I was pissed. I didn't care to be referred to as 'this one' as if I were a commodity.

"Why did you do that?" I asked. "Jason and I were really enjoying each other's company. I'm a big boy and that was totally uncalled for."

"Yes, it was," Monte said with a smile on his face. "Everyone here knows the rules of the house. The guy in my bedroom is off limits to everyone else. Do you understand?"

"I understand," I answered, "but I don't know if I like your house rule. Most of these guys are hot, hot, hot!"

"They are all hot," Monte said. "At one time or another every one of them has shared my bedroom at one of my parties." He sat down next to me where Jason had been, and he kissed my cock. Then he left me to go talk to the other guests.

Larry came over to me and told me what room he was in should I need anything during my stay. Then he rang a gong to get everyone's attention.

"Dinner will be served in one hour, at 8:30, in the dining room. You might wish to shower before dinner, but again clothing is optional. Should you choose not to dress, Monte has asked that you kindly bring a fresh, dry towel to place on your dining room chair. We'd like to avoid hash marks on the white upholstery." He said the last words with a smirk in his voice.

I went to Monte's room and ran into the shower. Since I am a creature of habit, I paid particular attention to my private area as I do every evening. While I was scrubbing my ass, the shower door opened and Monte came in. He enfolded me in his arms and began to kiss me on the lips. Little by little his lips descended down my body until his tongue was caressing my cock. Monte was a superb cock sucker and it didn't take me long to fill his mouth with my copious flow of jism. Monte swallowed every drop.

"That was good," he said. "You owe me one, and I'll collect when we turn in tonight."

"The pleasure will be all mine."

As we were drying each other off, I asked. "I didn't see any cooking going on. What's for dinner?"

"A catering truck will arrive any minute from *The Four Seasons* in Manhattan. If they didn't fuck up, we'll be having shrimp cocktail, Cornish hen with baked potatoes, an assortment of red wines and baked Alaska for dessert. They will also leave food for Saturday to Monday dinners. Larry will prepare breakfasts and lunches. After we dine tonight the other guests will spend the evening poolside for however long they want, but you and I are retiring after dinner for a sporting event of our own."

"That sounds good to me," I said and I fondled Monte's cock.

I put on a pair of boxer shorts and Monte looked at me questioningly.

"I don't like nudity around food," I said. I can't tolerate the vision of pubic hair alighting in my shrimp cocktail."

Monte laughed. He went to his dresser and took out a pair of briefs which he put on. We smiled at each other and went down to dinner.

I was amazed at the dinner conversation. To my surprise there was little or no talk about sex. The group seemed to be very intelligent. The main topic of discussion was current events, with a smattering of the two taboos, religion and politics. Occasionally everyone seemed to be talking at once and at other times one person was able to hold everyone else's attention. On a scale of one to ten, our dinner conversation would have rated a ten.

My trained eye was able to pick out one guest who seemed not to participate in the evening's proceedings. Chief Jason sat very quietly. His eyes never left off staring at Monte. There was venom in that stare, I swear. Monte seemed not to notice. I had to conclude that there must have been many times in the past that they had vied for the same prey. Was I someone's prey this evening? I could only wonder.

Almost everyone at the table was nude. Only a couple of other guests wore underwear or shorts like Monte and me. We had been served by the caterer's all male crew and as everyone got up to leave the table, the cleanup began immediately. Four guests had coupled off and each couple went to a bedroom just as Monte and I did. The rest went to the pool for a little more frolicking. Since the caterer was doing all the household chores, I noticed that Larry joined the other guests at the pool. Monte must have given him permission.

Back in our room, Monte locked the door and began to kiss me passionately. Our tongues brushed together sending shivers through my body. He led me to the bed and whispered, "You owe me. Pay up."

"Not so fast," I told him. With that I proceeded to give him a trip around the world. I didn't miss an inch of him, front or back. Of course, I stayed away from his cock and balls until he began to whimper and he begged me to take him. I took his cock in my hand and started to lick the head and his piss slit. Monte was whining like a baby. Finally I put him out of his misery. I enveloped his cock with my mouth. My tongue ran up and down his shaft and my lips ran alongside travelling with my tongue.

I sensed he would come soon and I stopped. "Where's your lube and condoms?" I asked.

"In the top drawer of my night table."

I reached into the drawer and pulled out a condom, which I rolled down Monte's cock. Then I greased his cock and my ass hole. I straddled Monte and lowered myself on his cock until he fully penetrated me. I began to push down on him as he thrust up to me. We tried to delay Monte's orgasm as long as possible, but finally he came screaming loudly. Eventually he softened and fell out of me. I let my body fall forward on top of him and we began to kiss.

We lingered for what seemed like forever, but at last we got up and went to the bathroom where we disposed of the condom and washed up as best we could. Finally we got back in bed, cuddled together and fell asleep.

Sometime in the middle of the night, I thought that I heard a thud against our bedroom door. I sighed uncomfortably, but Monte's arm was around me and I did not wish to wake him up so I just continued to sleep. About five in the morning I did wake up because I had to pee so badly. Monte was still asleep and snoring lightly. I crept out of bed to go to the bathroom. While I was peeing, I remembered what I thought was a dream, but I suddenly began to sense that it was no dream. I walked stealthily to the door so as not to disturb Monte. I unlocked it and I tried to open it.

The door opened out into the hall. As I pushed the door to open it, I was met with a great resistance. The door would not budge. I pushed harder and moved it a few inches. I kept at it until I had opened it enough to squeeze myself through.

There were several night lights in the hallway, enough for me to see that someone's wrists were bound with pillow cases, and then tied to the bedroom door handle. I had noticed where Larry had turned the hall lights on and off and I ran directly to the light switch. I turned it on without hesitating.

Someone was tied to the door handle as I described. He was naked and his body was turned to the floor. I went over and put my fingers on the victim's carotid artery. There was no discernable pulse. I turned the head and gasped. It was Abel and he was quite dead. His throat had been slit, but obviously it had been done elsewhere. There was no sign of any blood in the hallway.

Chapter Two

My first inclination was to summon Jason to the crime scene, or at least to the spot where the body had been dumped. I realized that I didn't know which room was his, but I knew which room was Larry's. I tried to be as quiet as possible so as not to awaken anyone. When I got to Larry's room, I tapped lightly.

There was no answer so I opened the door. Larry was lying in bed sound asleep. He was naked and the covers were thrown back. I approached him and by the light of a small night light, I saw immediately that there was dried semen in his pubic hairs. I looked further and could see several semen stains on the sheets. Obviously Larry had experienced a hot night. But where was his partner? Why was he alone? I shook his shoulder and tried to wake him, but was totally unsuccessful.

I switched on the lamp at his bedside and I pulled back one of his eyelids. His pupil should have been totally dilated but it was a mere pinpoint. Larry had taken drugs or had been drugged. I could not leave him like this. I am much bigger than he, so I just dragged him out of bed and started walking with him. We were stumbling together up and down the hall when suddenly he slurred, "What happened? My head is killing me."

"Where's Jason's room?" I asked. With great difficulty he raised his left hand as if it weighed a ton, and pointed to the third door ahead of us on the right. I struggled with him until we reached Jason's door. I didn't bother to knock, but went right in. Jason was sleeping wrapped up around Ian. I must have startled him because he woke with a jump and nearly threw Ian off the bed.

"Good God," the Chief said. "What's going on?"

I waved my head as if to say *follow me*. Ian just kept on sleeping.

I was still struggling with a semi-awake Larry, and Jason followed us out to the hall. "Look," I whispered, pointing my head towards Abel's body. "I think we better call the police."

"I *am* the police," he whispered. "I can't call anyone. If it got out that I was at this party, my career would be over. No. You and I will have to run the investigation, and until it's concluded nobody leaves this house. Is that understood?"

If I was dressed, I would have clicked my heels and yelled, *Jawohl, mein fuehrer.*

"I've got to continue walking Larry," I explained. "He's been drugged. Why don't you examine the body and see what you can find out."

"Are there any rubber gloves in the kitchen?" Jason asked the semi-comatose Larry.

"Under the sink," Larry slurred. Jason disappeared and returned shortly wearing bulky dishwashing gloves. He approached the victim and began to examine the body.

"His throat's been slashed," he announced.

"Doh!" I responded.

"He's got a bump on the back of his head the size of a baseball. The perp hit him hard with a heavy blunt object before he slit his throat or else he hit his head when he was dragged out of bed."

"Either the blow killed him or he was killed elsewhere and dragged back here. That would explain the lack of blood," I offered my opinion.

The body was positioned face down. Jason removed the ties from the door handle and turned the body on its back. "Oh God!" Jason gasped. "His cock's been cut off." I was still holding Larry up and walking him in circles. We both glanced at the corpse and I for one almost gagged, and remember I have seen everything.

"Other than the bump on his head, there are no other signs of trauma," the Chief said. He lifted one of Abel's eyelids. "He's been heavily drugged too," he stated. Then he stood up and took hold of Larry's other side.

"Why don't you walk Larry a little," I said to Jason. "His pupils are beginning to dilate somewhat. I think he's coming around. I better wake Monte and let him know what's going on. Let's try to figure out what we can do with the body. It's supposed to get into the high eighties today."

I opened Monte's bedroom door, closed it behind me, and went in. Monte was still snoring lightly. I tapped him on his shoulder and he stirred somewhat. I shook a little harder and he awakened. He looked at me, smiled and said, "I'm all done out. Please, no more sex until after breakfast."

'Monte," I said, "Brace yourself. One of your guests has been murdered. It's Abel." He looked at me with a blank stare on his face. It wasn't sinking in so I repeated. "Abel has been murdered."

Monte grabbed his head with both his hands and began to rock back and forth. "Oh my God! Oh my God!" he repeated over and over. Finally he jumped out of bed. "I've gotta pee," he said and ran to the bathroom. While he was peeing, I opened the bedroom door. Jason was still walking Larry around, but Larry seemed to be maneuvering quite well. I motioned for them to come into Monte's bedroom. They came into the bedroom carrying

Abel's lifeless body with them. When they came in, I closed the door again as Monte emerged from the bathroom.

They laid the body on a chaise lounge and covered it with Monte's comforter. Then they sat on the two boudoir chairs in the room, and Monte and I sat on the edge of the bed. I would say that this was the moment the investigation began and Jason took the helm. He looked at Monte and said, "Nobody leaves this house until we find the murderer. If it ever gets out that I was here at this party, I'll be sweeping floors backstage at one of your plays. Is that understood? I'll use my police authority to prevent anyone from leaving." He looked at me. "How did you come to discover the body?"

"In the middle of the night, or early morning, I'm not sure which, I thought I heard a thump against the door, but I was more asleep than awake and Monte had his arms around me. I didn't want to disturb him and I fell asleep again. About five, I got up to pee. I remembered the thud and decided to investigate. When I tried to open the door it wouldn't budge. I pushed and pushed until I finally had enough room to squeeze out, and that's when I discovered Abel's remains. I wanted to alert you, Chief, but I didn't know what room you were in, so I went to Larry's room.

"I knew he had slept with someone because there was dried semen on the sheets and in his pubic hair. When I tried to wake him up, I realized that he had used drugs, or been drugged, so I got him out of bed and started walking him around. He was already coming out of it and the walking helped. He led me to your room, and you know the rest."

"Larry," the chief asked, "who did you sleep with last night?"

Larry could only muster up a hoarse whisper. "Abel."

"Do you use drugs, Larry?" Jason asked, almost kindly.

"I did when I was a teen ager, but I swear I haven't even had a joint in over five years."

"Do you have any inkling as to when you might have been drugged?"

"Somebody could have put something in my drink at the pool before Abel and I turned in. But if that's the case, I want more of that stuff, because Abel and I had the most fantastic sex I ever had. Someone could have come into the room after we fell asleep and somehow drugged me. All I know is that when I fell asleep, Abel was alive and in bed with me. When Ken woke me up, he was dead in the hallway, and I was in a stupor. I can't tell you more. I don't remember anything between falling asleep and Ken waking me up. Oh God, help us all!"

As he spoke, I observed the others in the room. Jason was listening intently, obviously analyzing every word, every nuance in Larry's body. Monte was staring at Larry with a look I can only describe as a sneer. Frankly that surprised me. It appeared that Monte had already concluded that Larry had murdered Abel. After observing all the others, I asked Larry to stand in front of me. I examined his entire body, front and back, and then I saw it. He had a tiny little pin prick, which had caused the smallest of welts, on his left buttocks.

'When I found you, Larry, you were lying on your back. Do you ever sleep on your stomach?"

"Yes, I always fall asleep on my stomach."

"Of course," I replied, and motioned Jason over to look at the tiny welt. The Chief nodded, agreeing that was probably how the drug was administered.

The Chief resumed speaking. "After dinner, Barry and Elroy, Don and Francis, and Monte and Ken went off to their rooms together. I know that after the pool party, I went off with Ian, and Larry went off with Abel. That leaves Conrad, Grant and Harry unaccounted for."

"Since there is only one bedroom left," Monte interjected, "they must all be together."

"I think it would be a good idea, Ken, if you looked in all the bedrooms to see if everyone is accounted for." I hurried out of the room and peeked in to each of the bedrooms. Everyone was sound asleep, and indeed Conrad, Grant and Harry were a happy threesome.

"All present and accounted for," I reported back. "Now fellas, what are we going to do with the body?"

"We have a deep freeze in the basement," Larry offered. "There is some food in it, but I think I can get most of it into the kitchen freezer and maybe I can cook what's left."

"Let's get to work then before everybody gets up," I said. I threw the comforter off the body and grabbed its feet as Jason picked it up by the shoulders. When we got to the basement, we removed the food from the deep freeze and stuffed the body in it. We all helped bring the food upstairs and Larry put all but three packages of sirloin steaks in the freezer. "I'll barbeque these for dinner," he said. "The caterer's food is already frozen and is stacked in the freezer. I'll just use it another time."

"I'd better shower and then start breakfast," he said. "I imagine everyone will be waking up soon."

"That's a good idea," Jason said. "I think we should all freshen up. I'll tell everyone what happened at breakfast. After breakfast we can interview each of them individually," he said looking at me.

I showered as quickly as I could and put on a pair of gym shorts. I opened Monte's door a notch so that I could peer up the hallway to Larry's room. As soon as he left to start breakfast, I went into his room. Following right behind me was the Chief. "I guess we both have the same idea," he said.

"The crime began here so here's where we should look first," I concluded. We scoured every inch of the room, and found nothing, but that in and of itself was significant. If there was no sign of a scuffle, then probably Abel had been drugged prior to his being removed from the bed. That would indicate he and Larry both received the drug prior to leaving the pool, but yet the two men had experienced wonderful and wild sex. It didn't make

3 Erotic Gay Novellas

sense. It was more probable that they were drugged after sex, but how? I'd have to think about it. I voiced my thoughts aloud to Jason.

"Maybe the murderer paid them a visit. They knew everyone in the house and would not have kept anyone from entering their room. They may even have anticipated a three way," Jason commented.

"But Larry told us they came back to the room, had sex, fell asleep and that's all he remembered. He never mentioned a visitor, but he might still be hazy. We can ask him again later," I said.

When we were done going through Larry's room and all his belongings, we went to the other rooms and woke everyone up. There was much objection, but we told the guys that something had happened and they had to get their asses downstairs for breakfast.

When we got to the dining room, we were pleased to smell fresh coffee, along with fried and scrambled eggs and crisp bacon. A platter of assorted bagels and butter patties was laid out alongside the other food on a long server. Little by little the dining room table filled and everyone had a plate of food in front of them. I asked Monte to summon Larry from the kitchen. When he came in, he made himself a breakfast plate and joined us at the table. One chair at the table was empty.

"Where's Abel," Grant asked

"That's why we're here," Jason said. "Now listen up." Jason slowly and meticulously related the events of the morning and Abel's murder to the assembled group. They were all aghast, but Francis jumped up and said, "I'm out of here."

"Nobody leaves," Jason said emphatically. "I'm the police chief and the murder occurred in my jurisdiction. Anyone who leaves this house, before we find the killer, will be arrested on suspicion of murder. Is that clear?"

Francis sat down in defeat.

"After breakfast Ken and I will be interviewing each one of you," Jason informed them. "You may have seen or heard something which seemed of no consequence at the time but which might be very important in light of what has happened. So while you are waiting to be questioned, put on your thinking caps. Did you hear or see anything which would shed some light on this affair?"

Monte had a small study which housed his desk and two chairs facing the desk. Jason and I decided that this was an ideal place for the interviews. We started with Larry, who raised holy hell, complaining that he had to pick up the dishes, put them in the dishwasher, dispose of the leftovers and clean up the dining room. Actually he had been clearing the table all through breakfast, and there wasn't that much left to do.

"You've already given me the third degree," he protested.

"Relax partner," I tried to soothe him. "We only have another question or two to ask you. Between the time you entered your room and fell asleep, did you have any visitors at all?"

"Actually yes," Larry answered. "I was dab smack in the middle of being fucked by Abel, when Harry walked in without even knocking. He asked if I had some aspirin and I told him he could find a bottle in the top drawer of my night table. He took some and left. I had forgotten all about it. It's not something you place priority memory on when you are in the middle of being fucked, and then your fuck buddy gets murdered afterward."

"OK," I said. "That's all we wanted to know. Would you send Harry in next?"

Harry could shed little light on the situation but we did ask if he had left his room at any time during the night.

"Yes," he said. "I had a terrible hangover so I went to Larry's room to ask where I could get some aspirin. He and Abel were fucking, but Larry was still able to direct me to a drawer containing a bottle of aspirin. I took a few pills and left. When I left Larry's room, Abel was alive and more than kicking."

We interviewed the guys one at a time and learned nothing. Nobody had seen or heard anything. When we were through with each of them, we sent them to the pool to hang out, and have some fun if they could. All the interviews were completed and Jason was ready to throw in the towel.

"Not yet, Chief," I said. "We haven't interviewed Barry."

"That's right. I guess I lost count," he said.

"I'll go get him," I said. I had expected him to be waiting outside the study, but he wasn't there. I went into the dining room, where I found Larry vacuuming the floor. He was pushing the vacuum with his left hand and it was the first time I realized that he was left handed. The needle prick was on his left buttock. It could have been self-inflicted.

"Have you seen Barry?" I asked him.

"No! Isn't he with the other guys?" Larry asked.

"I'll go to the pool and see if he's there," I said.

"Has anyone seen Barry?" I yelled out. They all shook their heads. I ran back to Jason and practically screamed, "Barry's skipped out. He must be our man."

"Don't panic," Jason said. "Maybe he's in the house. Let's check out the bedrooms." We ran upstairs and proceeded to check out every bedroom. In the second bedroom I looked, I found Barry asleep on the bed. He had come to breakfast naked and he was still naked. He was lying on his stomach. I went over to rouse him only to discover that Barry was as dead as Abel, but at least his cock had not been lopped off. I wasn't having much fun this weekend, finding dead bodies all over the place. I went out into the hall and saw the chief. I waved for him to come into Barry's room.

"He's dead," I said very matter of factly. "There's an odor around his mouth that smells like arsenic. What do you think, Chief?"

"It definitely smells like a poison, but I don't know if it's arsenic. What the fuck are we going to do now?"

Chapter Three

Jason and I stared at each other in disbelief. Not only was there a murderer in the house, he was a serial killer to boot. This was hardly the fun-filled, sex-filled weekend either of us had envisioned.

"This better stop happening," Jason said. "There's only room for this one body, and no more, in the deep freeze."

We weren't even going to bother to examine the body. It was obvious that poison was the murder weapon. But our training did require that we take a cursory look at the corpse. I saw it first.

"Look there, Chief," I said. "He's got a tiny needle prick on the back of his neck. He was either injected with poison or forced to swallow it after the contents of the needle disabled him. Let's get him into the freezer while the others are all at the pool and then we'll have to do the interviews again," I said. Then as an afterthought I added, "But Chief, some of the guys are going to want to bolt out of here and I don't see how we can stop them."

"I'll be forced to have them arrested on suspicion of murder. I'd hate to do that, but I'll have to, and I'll have to face the music about my being here," the chief lamented.

"Not necessarily," I consoled him. "We can make sure everybody gets dressed, and as far as the community at large is concerned, a bunch of bachelors were having a pool party."

"It's a stretch," Jason sighed but we don't have many options, and I can't ignore my duty as a police officer."

"Nor can I," I added quickly. "Now let's freeze the body until we can get an autopsy performed."

We carried Barry's body down the stairs and as we reached the bottom, I heard a little screech. I had forgotten that Larry was in the kitchen and he could see us. He ran over to see who we were carrying and screamed again. "Oh my God, it's Barry. Is he dead?"

"Yes," I answered. "Now help us get him into the deep freeze with Abel."

We had to really push hard to get the freezer cover shut, even after laying the bodies in a sixty-nine position. I told Larry to get back to his duties, whatever it was he was doing, and Jason and I went out to join the other men at the pool. The sight which awaited me was the opposite of what I saw yesterday. Nobody was in the pool. To a man, they were seated on chairs and lounges around the pool talking in hushed tones. That made it easy for the chief to address them.

"Listen guys," Jason began, "there has been another murder."

I heard a collective gasp. "It's Barry this time," the chief said. Elroy screamed.

"No, it's not possible," he cried. "We fucked each other just a few hours ago. I'm sorry. I can't stay here another minute. I'm leaving and there's nothing you can do to stop me."

"Yes I can," Jason said. "I can have every one of you arrested on suspicion of murder. Now sit down and listen to me. This whole matter is more than out of hand. I want you all to go to your rooms and get dressed. Then I'm going to call in the police. As far as anyone is concerned we are a bunch of bachelors at a Labor Day pool party and barbeque. No one is going to utter a single word about sex. Is that clear? That way we can have the bodies removed for autopsy. You will all be questioned, but at least you'll be released on bond until you are needed again."

"Yes, yes, do that," Ian said. "Then at least we can have some police protection and get our sorry asses home."

We were all glad to get dressed and start the process of a full blown police investigation. We hurried to our rooms, got dressed, and packed our few clothes in anticipation of a quick ride out of this hell. I think I was the first one downstairs.

I suddenly realized that I was parched, so I went into the kitchen to get a cold drink. The kitchen was empty and I assumed that Larry had gone upstairs to dress. But if he did, who told him to do so. He was nowhere near the pool when the order to dress was issued. Still, the house wasn't so big that he could not have been informed by someone.

This time the men gathered in the living room. Monte took a head count. "Where's Conrad?" he asked. Conrad had shared a room with Grant and Harry, so Harry spoke up. "He had to take a crap and said that he would be right down."

"Where's Larry?" I asked.

"In the kitchen as far as I know," Monte answered. I took a quick trip to the kitchen and Larry was indeed there, preparing lunch. I returned to the living room just as Jason pulled out his cell phone and called his next in command. The chief walked into another room but I could hear him giving muffled instructions to whoever he was talking to.

"There will be two detectives here in fifteen or twenty minutes," he told us. "So sit tight." We all sat down in total silence. Not a word was spoken for about five minutes when suddenly Jason blurted out, "For God sakes, how long does it take to dump a load?" He looked straight at Harry. "Go see what's taking Conrad so long will you?" he ordered Harry, who rushed upstairs.

It was only a moment or two later when we heard a blood curdling scream. Harry started to yell, "Jason, Jason, come up here on the double." Everyone ran upstairs, but they allowed Jason and I to enter Conrad's room first.

"In the bathroom!" I heard Harry instruct us. Jason ran in first and I was close behind him. He stopped short and I nearly knocked him down. There was Conrad in the bathtub. The bathtub was full of water and Conrad's head was below the waterline, an apparent drowning victim. In light of the circumstances nobody could believe this was a drowning accident. The conclusion was obvious, MURDER!

"OK everyone," Jason yelled. "I want you all back downstairs immediately and in the living room. We'll wait for my men there. In the meantime don't go anywhere or do anything unless someone is with you. Never let yourself go solo anywhere and that includes the bathroom. Is that understood?" To a man they all nodded their heads.

"Ken, you stay here with me and help me with the body," the chief said.

We drained the tub and dried the body as best we could. Then we lifted him out of the tub and on to the bed. We examined the body and found the tell tale pin prick on the back of his neck. Jason covered him with a sheet and we were about to go downstairs when I said, "Jason, we have to protect Don."

"Why Don?" Jason asked.

"The guys are getting murdered alphabetically. The first victim was Abel, then Barry and now Conrad," I forced Jason to observe.

"That could be a mere coincidence," Jason said. "If you are correct, you and I are the last two victims and Monte is the murderer."

"I am Monte's alibi, at least for Abel. There is no way Monte murdered Abel, unless he has an assistant. Besides, I can't imagine what his motive would be. And if he was planning a weekend murder spree, why invite two cops? On the very first night, the murderer could have gone from room to room and done away with each of the inhabitants in his sleep. Why is he working it one corpse at a time? Frankly nothing makes sense to me," I complained.

Jason agreed with me and we went downstairs and headed for the living room. It took Jason and me about two seconds to realize that Don was not in the room.

"Where the fuck is Don?" the chief screamed. "I told you nobody is to go solo.

"He was right behind me on the stairway," Grant observed. "I am so upset, I didn't realize he was gone."

I pulled Jason aside. "Remember when we took Barry's body downstairs, Larry spotted us from the kitchen. He was in the kitchen when the others came downstairs. I have a terrible feeling."

"You guys stay here in the living room. If someone needs to go to the bathroom, take another man along with you. That's an order," Jason said.

He and I left the room and headed for the kitchen. We had to pass the foot of the stairs and from there we could see Larry washing some serving trays. I had a hunch and walked around the staircase. As is often the case in older homes there was a door to a storage area on the side of the stair case. I tried to open it but it was locked.

I went into the kitchen and asked Larry if he had a key to the storage closet under the staircase. "All the keys are on a key rack in the mud room," he said. "I'll get it for you." He returned quickly with the key and the three of us opened the door. As soon as we did, Don's body tumbled out. A large kitchen knife protruded from the victims back.

"Shit and shit again," Jason muttered. "I can't even prevent a murder under my own nose." He took out his handkerchief and removed the knife from the body. "Get me a big plastic bag for the knife, and a table cloth to cover

Don with," he ordered a sniveling Larry, who did as he was asked. By now the others were gathered around us and most were sobbing and crying. Monte was the worst of them.

"How could this happen to me?" he cried over and over.

We hustled everyone into the living room and I yelled to Larry, "Forget the fucking kitchen jobs. You stay with us." Then I yelled at Elroy, "And you, don't leave my side. Attach yourself to my hip and stay there. Is that understood?" Elroy nodded numbly at me.

I counted heads and all the survivors were accounted for. We found seats in the living room and everyone sat quietly waiting for Jason's men to show up. I didn't realize it at first, but I was holding Elroy's hand tightly, and he was sobbing. "I'm so thirsty," he said.

Larry jumped up. "I'll get you some water," he said.

"Sit your sorry ass down," I commanded. In my head Larry was the prime suspect. He had once shared Monte's bed only to be replaced by all these others, and he was one jealous dude.

I was still holding Elroy's hand and I took him into the kitchen with me. I opened the fridge and found a pitcher of Crystal Lite. I poured him a glassful which he gulped down, and I took him back into the living room. When we got back, Elroy said that he had to pee.

Remembering Jason's instructions, Francis said that he would take him to the bathroom. I wasn't about to let *E* and *F* go off together so I said, "Sorry Francis, no way. Ian, you go with Elroy." I figured that the letter *I* was far enough away from the letter *E*. "Don't let go of him for a second," I ordered Ian. "I don't care if you have to hold his cock while he pees. Is that understood?" They both nodded and headed for the john.

Just as Elroy and Ian returned to the living room, the doorbell rang, and Larry went to answer it. He let in two very ordinary looking men who shook the chief's hand. Then the three of them went into a huddle. One of the two detectives pulled out his cell phone and made a whispered call.

"They're sending for ambulances to remove the bodies and take them to the county morgue. I don't think there's enough vaults for all of them. We may have to use a local mortuary also," Jason said.

The two detectives looked around the room. They were eying the half-naked hunks and neither had any doubt as to the true nature of the gathering. I couldn't tell anything about what one of the detectives was thinking, but the other had a look of sheer disgust on his face. I couldn't help wonder what he was thinking about his boss.

Finally, one of the detectives addressed the assembled suspects including me and the chief. "After the bodies are removed, I'm sending for four cars to take you all down to the station, two to a car. You can ride down with us, Chief. Every one of you (he looked directly at the chief and then at me) are under arrest on suspicion of murder." He read us our rights and informed us that we could call an attorney from the station house. This was definitely not the weekend I had signed up for.

The media shamelessly pay cops to inform them of breaking news. As a result, Monte's place was swarming with TV and newspaper reporters as the bodies were being removed. By the time we were all being placed in police cars, there were even more of them. I chose to ride with Elroy. I still worried that he was the next victim. He cried the whole trip down and leaned into me. He placed his hand on my crotch, I guess for comfort, and I actually got hard.

As for me, I called one of the best public defenders I had ever met in my years as a detective in New York. He had difficulty believing my story, but agreed to come up to Nyack first thing Tuesday morning. I forgot about the holiday. It looked like we would be languishing in jail for the rest of today, Sunday and Monday morning. We couldn't even hope for a judge to set bail for us.

We were each assigned separate cells. *No more hanky-panky this weekend,* I thought. Each cell had one barred window so at least we could enjoy some outside sunlight. Monte was on one side of me and Jason was on the other.

I was a bit surprised that Jason was considered a suspect by his staff, and I questioned him about it.

"I insisted that we all have equal treatment, and that includes me and you," he explained to me. "Just because we are peace officers doesn't give us immunity from suspicion."

That night, as we were preparing for sleep, I could hear crying and sobbing coming from the various cells. I really felt sorry for these guys. They were frightened and feared for their lives. I am sure that none of them had ever seen the inside of a jail before. I glanced across the hall and I could see that Harry and Francis had put their arms through the bars and were holding hands to comfort each other. I don't know why but I suddenly felt like a mother hen to a bunch of little chicks. I felt a duty to protect them. That desire sent a warm feeling through my body and for the first time in a long time I fell sound asleep without sex and without whacking off. However, my trained ear did hear the sound of jerking off from other cells.

About four o'clock in the morning, I heard a terrible commotion. I jumped off my cot and could see two guards peering into Elroy's cell. Elroy was two cells down from me on the other side of Monte and I couldn't see a thing, but Harry across the hall yelled out, "He's dead! He's covered with blood."

I was thunderstruck. What now? All the suspects were locked up in their cages, so it could not have been any one of the incarcerated men. Could someone, who was not at the party, be the one committing the murders? That was a strong possibility. Now it was my turn to have an overwhelming desire. I longed to question the police officers on duty at the jail this night. They were now prime suspects to a murder along with the rest of us.

As the body was being removed, Jason said, "Ken, can you hear me?"

"Yes," I answered.

"This latest murder kind of lets us all off the hook," Jason said. "I've never had a case like this one in my whole life."

"Neither have I," I had to admit. "Neither have I. Do you know how he was murdered?"

"Yes, one of the guards told me," the chief answered. "He was stabbed in the chest, and once again his penis was lopped off."

"God, this is so gruesome and so bizarre," I managed to respond.

Chapter Four

"Chief," I whispered through the bars. "We have to question the night guards. Unless they were asleep or unless they are the murderers, they must have heard something."

"You're right," he said. "I'll call them." He whipped out his cell phone and I thought that rank indeed has its privileges. The cops had confiscated the cell phones from the rest of us.

In a moment the Chief and I were released from our cells and taken to the front office. As we left, I could hear the moans and groans of the rest of the men. There were two officers on duty and they were useless in shedding any light on the matter. They informed us that one or the other of them had checked the cells every hour on the hour. The duty officer had shined his flashlight on everyone as he passed the cell. Elroy's body was discovered at 4 AM. The duty officer called for his companion. They administered CPR to no avail. They called the medical examiner who arranged to have the body removed to the morgue for autopsy. Both of them swore that they had seen nothing and heard nothing, and that nobody could get into the cell without a key.

They returned Jason and me to our cells where we both tried to get a little rest before breakfast. I lay down on the cot and tried to piece things together. Back at the house, my prime suspect was Larry. He had motive and opportunity in each instance of murder. But he acted like a sniveling coward each time a body was discovered. It occurred to me that if he worked for Monte, he might well be an actor, and if so, he was a damned good one. But Larry had no opportunity to murder Elroy in this jail. That made Jason my chief suspect. He had been allowed to keep his cell phone, or if that was not the case, his men had not searched him and he simply retained it. If he had the phone, maybe he had a key to the cells. If he had a key, then he became a prime suspect. But how did he get a knife?

So where did that put me? Nowhere! Perhaps Jason and Larry were in cahoots with each other. That could well be. Both were pissed that Monte had replaced them in his bedroom, and the chief resented that Monte kept his current bed partner off limits to everyone else. The more I thought about it, the more sense it made.

As for the victims they were real innocents. They had come out to the country for a sex filled weekend. They knew that they could have sex with anyone at the party. They would never suspect that anyone coming anywhere near them, would have intentions of murder. I shuddered at the thought, and my heart went out to the victims, and to the rest of us intended victims. I vowed to get little or no sleep until I was out of this place. I lay awake grasping every little sound and trying to interpret it.

Soon the cell block began to lighten, heralding another sunny, warm Sunday morning. The morning watch arrived with trays of food, and announced that the prison chaplain would arrive soon and would hold a Sunday Service for those of us who cared to attend. Strangely, everyone felt the need to attend, even Harry, who was a Muslim. His real name was Hareem.

After a pitiful breakfast (considering yesterday's gourmet feast) the guards escorted us to a small chapel. The chaplain this morning was Father Flynn, a Roman Catholic priest. There was some mumbling from the group because there was not a catholic among us. Father Flynn began to laugh. "You'll have to put up with me today," he said. "Last week Rabbi Cohen conducted the service." The men laughed and relaxed, and the priest gave a modified service that could offend nobody, not even Harry. I don't know if the good Father was clued in or not, but his homily that morning concerned the commandment that we shall not commit murder, and the story of Cain and Abel. I wondered if Father Flynn was aware that the first victim was named Abel. I looked around and could not see that anyone was fidgeting in his seat.

When the service came to a close, Father Flynn blessed us, wished us well, and left to serve mass at his own church. The guards told us to stand and march out single file. We all stood, except Francis. He was seated two spaces to my left. Larry was between us.

"You," one of the guards yelled at Francis, "stand up."

Francis did not move so Larry nudged his shoulder and he fell over, knocking down three chairs along the way. I rushed over and could clearly smell the same poison that I had smelled on Barry. I had begun to grab the body, but when I smelled the poison, I stopped dead in my tracks. One of the guards ran over to assess the situation.

"Take the rest back to their cells and lock them up good and tight," he yelled to his co-worker. "This one's dead."

Back in my cell, I tried hard to think through this new turn of events. Our breakfast trays were served to us individually in our cells. The only people who could have tampered with the meals were the preparers and/or the servers. Could Jason have a whole army of coconspirators? It boggled my mind. Anyway, I really had no evidence to link Jason to the murders. It was all just a hunch, and my hunch included Larry also. What if I was barking up the wrong tree? What if it was someone else entirely, and I was missing all the evidence? *Think hard,* I kept telling myself. *There are only three more possible victims before Chief Jason, and then I'm next.*

As was to be expected, every remaining one of us refused our lunch trays. Actually, the only one in immediate danger was Grant. I wondered if we could all go hungry for two more days. Did we dare trust the water? I was beginning to get more and more miserable. After what would have been our lunch break, we were all escorted into a court yard. There we could enjoy the beautiful day and toss around a baseball. We were grateful for the recreation time, although I would have preferred hanging out at Monte's pool.

The best part of the walk to the courtyard was that we passed a water fountain in the hallway. I had seen guards drinking from the fountain so I did not hesitate to quench my thirst. Once I did that, everyone followed suit.

In the courtyard Harry and I started to jog in a tight circle. The space we had was rather limited. Monte sat down on a small bench and turned his face to the sun. His eyes were puffy and red. The murders, especially those in his own home, had really gotten to him. Grant, Larry, Ian and Jason went to the four corners of the yard. They began to toss a baseball. One of the guards had provided mitts and a hard ball. I laughed inwardly thinking that wasn't the hard ball they had in mind late Friday afternoon.

I was in great shape and before I even began to breathe hard, Harry gave up on jogging. He pushed Monte over and filled the rest of the small bench. I continued to jog, but desperately instructed my peripheral vision to be vigilant.

Finally, I gave up jogging, not because I was tired, but because I didn't want to lose sight of anyone in the courtyard. I sat down on the ground at the feet of the two men on the bench. We watched the guys tossing the ball, our heads following the ball all around the courtyard. It occurred to me that I shouldn't be doing that. I should be trying to keep my eyes on all four of them at once, but even watching three of them at one time was difficult.

When Grant fell, I only saw it out of the corner of my eye, but I did see it. He was two men away from receiving the ball. Suddenly his head snapped backwards and he fell. Jason and I ran right over, followed by a prison guard, but the others were frozen in disbelief. Grant was lying on his back and his face was a bloody sight. A small pellet protruded from his right eye. I wanted to vomit.

It was beginning to look more and more like the murderer was not Monte, Larry or any of the guests. As the guards removed Grant's body, I looked around the courtyard. Three sides were walled and all three walls were heavily treed, affording total privacy. The fourth wall wasn't a wall at all. It was the prison itself. The prison was three stories in all. The bottom two floors had no windows, but there were windows on the third floor. I asked the chief if there were offices on that level and he affirmed that there were.

"Somebody could have shot a dart from any of those windows," I said to the Chief. "If you were at the center window, you would have a clear view and a clear shot to the four corners of the yard where the guys tossing the baseball were standing."

"Are you saying that one of my men is a serial killer?" Jason asked me incredulously.

"Jason," I answered, "Nothing makes sense so anything is possible. You and I need to go unto a huddle with Monte. Like they say it's time for the truth and nothing but the truth. Please arrange it with your staff."

Out came Jason's cell phone again, and in just a few minutes, he, I and Monte were taken to a small interrogation room. As soon as we were comfortably seated, the guard left us alone and secured the door to the room.

"May I go first, Chief? I need to ask Monte some questions which hopefully will shed some light on this whole mess. You can fire away after me," I said.

"Sure." the chief said, and I began.

"Monte, who had access to your guest list?"

"Just Larry and me. Why do you ask?"

I ignored Monte's question and proceeded. "What about the person who did the calligraphy?" I asked. I could see that Monte became visibly upset.

"Anything wrong?" I asked him.

"No, no, I just forgot about him. I'm sorry I can't reveal his identity."

"You'll bloody well reveal it, or I'll have you arrested on seven counts of murder," the chief yelled at Monte.

"You can't do that," Monte sobbed. "I'm not a murderer."

"Maybe not, but maybe the fancy guy who addressed your invitations is."

Monte looked at me. His eyes were pleading. I was not sympathetic and I let him know. Why was he protecting this guy? Did Monte have feelings for this possible killer?

"You'd better tell us," I said or we can hold you for accessory to murder and suspicion of murder. You're in deep shit, Monte, so speak."

Monte grabbed his head between his hands and shook his head back and forth. "How could this be happening to me?" he sobbed.

"Talk!" the chief said ferociously.

Monte looked straight into Jason's eyes. "The man who did the calligraphy is Norman Sharpe," he murmured. Jason gasped.

"Who's Norman Sharpe?" I asked.

"Norman is one of my deputies. He's one of the two that came to the house yesterday. Is he one of your conquests?" he disdainfully asked Monte.

"It's more like I'm one of his," Monte hissed back. "We met in a gay bar in Manhattan about a year ago. We recognized each other from Nyack. Norm had come into town by bus and I offered to drive him back home. He ended up begging me to let him spend the night with me, and he spent many more nights to come."

"So," the chief said, "by letting him address the invitations to your weekend affair, you outed me."

"I swear Jason, I never thought about that. I even told him that I couldn't invite him because it was a business party, and that just business associates from the city would be there. I thought that he was cool with that."

"Has he ever indicated to you that he wanted a committed relationship or that he was jealous of your other bedmates?" I asked.

"No never, I swear. Norm is married and has a slew of kids." I looked at Jason and he nodded at me. I could appreciate why Monte wanted to protect Norm on many levels.

"Chief," I said, "I'd like to talk to Larry again. I have some more questions." The chief was really very obliging. He took out his cell phone and in no time a guard brought Larry in and took Monte out.

Larry looked at us very belligerently. "What the fuck! How many times are you going to question me? I'm scared shitless as it is and I don't feature being a suspect," he screamed at us.

"Like it or not," I said, "You are a suspect. Now tell me, how well do you know Norman Sharpe?"

"Well enough," Larry answered. "He was a frequent guest at the house and I served him more than one breakfast. That's as far as it went. He was a guest in Monte's bed, and as you both well know that put him out of bounds for me."

"Did he come around to the house anytime since Friday afternoon?" I asked.

"Yes, of course," Larry answered. "He was one of the two men who answered your initial call, Chief. As far as I know that was the only time he came around to the house."

Jason got on his cell phone again. He was speaking to one of his men. "I know Norm is off today, but find him and tell him to get his ass down to the jail ASAP. Thanks, and come get Larry will you."

Just as a guard came to take Larry back to his cell, Jason's phone rang. He listened intently and then hung up.

"Norm's wife said that he went fishing with some buddies. She doesn't expect him home until late tomorrow. The guard tried Norm's cell phone and it's turned off," he informed me. Then as an afterthought, "I'll bet he and his buddies are not doing a hell of a lot of fishing, except maybe up their asses."

One of the guards came back in the room and suggested that we allow him to take us back to our cells. The courtyard was now a crime scene and we survivors were more or less confined to quarters. Back in my cell, I fell back on my cot and attempted to sleep. I must have finally dozed off because I had an erotic dream. *It was Friday night and Monte was fucking my face. I knew from his sighs that he was enjoying my technique. I was pleasuring him and that pleasured me.*

When I awoke I could tell by the sunlight that it was late afternoon. My cock was outside my underwear and I was stroking it. I was about to cum so I pulled down my shorts, and I let it happen. There was a sink, soap and a towel in each cell and I used those items to clean myself.

As I was doing that I could tell that there was a lot of whispering going on in Jason's cell. I quickly put on my gym shorts and my tank top just as a guard opened my cell door and beckoned me to come with him.

I found myself back in the interrogation room with Jason and two guards. They all looked pretty grim. "What now?" I asked.

"Tell him Jim," Jason instructed.

"Harry called me to his cell about an hour ago. He asked if he could get a small area carpet that he could use as a prayer rug. He wanted to be taken to the chapel where he could perform afternoon prayers. He told me that he had long ago abandoned his religion, but in light of the events of the last two days, he felt a strong need for prayer. I took him to the chapel. I don't know the protocol for Muslim prayer so I left him alone. There's only one door to the chapel so I closed it and stood guard outside. I had no idea how long his prayers should last so after about twenty minutes, when he still had not come out, I went to investigate."

"Don't tell me," I said.

"Yes, you guessed it. His throat was slit and he was a goner. I searched every bit of the chapel. There was nobody there and no means of entrance or exit except for the door where I stood guard. It was one thing for the murderer to succeed in his heinous endeavors in Monte's mansion, but so many murders right here in jail, that's mind boggling." Jim faced Jason. "We're in deep shit," he said.

"This is sad, Jason," I said. "We actually played right into the murderer's hands this time. Whoever he is, he must have figured the one place that would not be used any more today was the chapel so he hid there. Obviously Harry was his next victim, and we conveniently delivered the boy to him. Nobody was supposed to be left alone, and it happened."

"It's not going to happen again," the chief said emphatically. "Jim, move another cot into my cell, and move Ian in. Then put another cot in Ken's cell and move Larry in there. That will leave Monte alone, but he's last on the list, if he is on the list. So watch his cell extra carefully."

Jim was about to leave when Jason said, "And keep on trying to reach Norm, will you?"

Chapter Five

I found myself alone in my cell with Larry. He had stripped to his Bikini shorts and was lying on his side facing me. He was trying to entice me and I must admit he is a tasty little morsel. I sure could have used a little sex and I thought that maybe we could do something tonight after lights out.

In the meantime I decided to put him completely at ease, so I used the Peter Falk, "Colombo" method of interrogation, which is no interrogation at all. Colombo allowed his suspects to talk freely until they hung themselves.

"That's a nice package you've got there," I observed.

"You like?" Larry asked, as he pulled his cock and balls out of the Bikini.

"I like a lot," I answered.

"You want? You're not in Monte's bed anymore. We are allowed to do each other," Larry let me know.

"I like and I want," I answered. "Later, after lights out."

Larry smiled at me. He stood up and sat down beside me on my cot. His hand rested on my knee and began to slide up and down my inner thigh.

He could see that I was getting hard and his hand began to caress my cock through my gym shorts. I leaned over and kissed him. As I did that he parted his lips and his tongue parted mine. I must admit that I liked the way he kissed, and I found myself hoping that he had nothing to do with the whole affair, but I was sure that he did.

"By the way," I said in my best Colombo manner. "Did you ever see Norman Sharpe naked?"

"Oh sure. I served him and Monte breakfast in bed often. He has the fattest, longest uncut cock I have ever seen. You can bet I was jealous of Monte."

"Did he ever come around to the house to see you during the week when Monte was in the city?"

I could tell in an instant that the last question made Larry uncomfortable. He shifted on the cot, turned slightly away so that his eyes were no longer facing me and said, "No, he never came around when Monte wasn't there." He was lying. After all my years of experience as a detective, his lie was a no brainer.

I poked him in his ribs with my elbow, and started to giggle. "Come on," I said. "How could he resist a good looking guy like you? I know I sure can't." I leaned over and kissed him on the cheek. Larry started to giggle also.

"Well, actually he did. Please don't tell Monte." I shook my head vigorously and laid my hand on his cock. What I was hoping for was happening. Larry was forgetting that I was a cop, and he began to confide in me. Now I must confide in you. Larry had the cutest smile I have ever seen and a beautiful body. His cock was cut, solid and smooth and I was beginning to drool. I was starting to get feelings for Larry, and I had to keep reminding myself that he might be a murderer and I better keep my mind on business.

"How often did the horny bastard come around?" I asked.

Larry smiled sheepishly and said, "Two or three times a week after work, and sometimes after dinner."

"I'm jealous," I said sincerely. I pulled Larry to me and began to kiss him passionately. To my joy, he was returning my kisses just as passionately. We were interrupted by the sound of dinner trays being rolled into the cell block. I found out later that in the next cell Jason and Ian were also resuming their activities of Friday night. I didn't realize it at the time, but I was falling in love, and hoped that something was happening between Ian and the handsome Chief of Police. I guess you think that way when you are in a romantic mood.

I really wasn't worried about there being poison in our food. Larry and I had two potential victims in front of us and both of them were in the next cell. I had to applaud Jason. Before he and Ian ate dinner, one of his men brought in a K-9 dog. Jason put a little food from his and Ian's trays in a dog dish, and offered it to the dog. He sniffed it and then devoured the food, looking for more.

After dinner, Larry and I did not wait for lights out to begin making love. From the sounds coming from the next cell, Jason and Ian were similarly occupied. I could only wonder what Monte was thinking. This time it was he who was left out.

We had no lube so we contented ourselves with oral sex. This evening, I forgot that I only did that for foreplay. Larry's cock felt so good against my tongue. It was so soft on the outside, yet I could feel the hardness on the inside. I couldn't get enough of him. When he came the first time, I kept right on sucking over his objection. In time the sensitivity disappeared and the passion returned. He came a second time in my mouth as he thanked me profusely over and over again. When he recovered, he returned the favor. Larry was a super cock sucker and I came rather quickly. However once was enough for me. I am a good fifteen years older than Larry, and I suppose that made the difference.

We tried to snuggle together on one cot, but it was just too small, and we finally had to reluctantly separate and get into separate cots.

"Goodnight, sweet," I whispered to Larry. I almost said that I loved him, but I forced myself to realize that he was a murder suspect. I was finding it harder and harder to believe that this sensitive young man could murder anything more than a chicken. Still he was a prime suspect.

We were awakened by the morning light. I yelled out to everyone and was relieved to learn that all five of us were still alive. We all had to pee and some of us needed to shit. Ian and Monte were taken to the latrine together and each made sure that they were in full sight of each other the whole time. When Ian had to dump a load, Jason made him leave the stall door open.

Monte went next accompanied by a guard and finally Larry and I went together. We peed and both of us shit in full view of the other. I never did that with any other living being except when I was in the navy. I respect the privacy of certain acts, and wish the same for others. Somehow, these bodily functions became a final form of intimacy between Larry and me. Before we left the head, we embraced and Larry said those fateful words.

"I think I've fallen in love with you." Before I could answer he pressed his lips on mine and prevented me from saying anything.

Back in our cell, I kissed him again and sat him down next to me. "Listen to me," I said in as serious a voice as I possibly could. "You are a prime suspect in the killings that occurred in the house. If you want me to protect you, you've got to be totally honest and tell me everything you know. I love you, Larry. Be honest with me so I can help you out of this mess and hopefully keep us both from becoming victims."

Larry threw his arms around me and began to cry. "Ken, Kenny," he sobbed, "I didn't kill anyone. I couldn't do that. I swear that's the truth. I can't lie to you, either. You're the man I love." He started planting wet and slobbery kisses all over my face. I pulled him to me and began to caress the back of his head. His blond hair was soft and silky like a young child's, and an overwhelming need to protect him overtook me. His erection was rubbing against me, and I was consumed with a warm glow of love. The feeling was overwhelming. I had never been in love before. *Please God*, I prayed. *Let him be telling me the truth.*

I held him for a while, reluctant to let go, afraid I would lose this glowing feeling. Finally we sat down on my cot together. I held his hand and said, "Think carefully. Take your time and tell me everything you can about Norman. Right now he's another prime suspect."

Larry put his head on my shoulder and I melted away. *Please be real,* I thought. *Don't be leading me on.*

Larry began: "One night I heard Monte's car pulling into the garage. Most of the time I'm a light sleeper. I didn't expect him until the next morning, so I got up to investigate. I saw him come in the front door with Norman. It was the first time I had ever laid eyes on him. I didn't know he was a cop until much later. I hate to tell you this, Kenny (I loved the way he called me Kenny), but I was pissed as hell. Usually when Monte got home, he called me right to his bed, but obviously it was not to be this time. I went back to my room, whacked off, and fell asleep."

Larry paused and looked at me. I think he wanted to see what my reaction would be to his having whacked off. "Relax, sweetheart, (I really called him that) I whack off all the time. As a lover I never disappoint myself." We both broke out laughing when I said that.

"I hope I never disappoint you," Larry said and I shook my head to let him know that he never could. He continued.

"In the morning, I brought them breakfast in bed. I knocked on Monte's door and he allowed me to enter. They were lying naked in bed, kissing and feeling themselves up. When I saw Norman's muscled body, I got a hardon myself. He must have noticed it because he winked at me.

"After breakfast, Norm showered and got dressed. He said he had to go to work, and he called for a cab. I never asked what kind of work he did. As I let him out the front door he pinched my ass and whispered to me, 'I'll see you again, little friend, when the cat's away. Then we mice will play.' "

Larry kept pausing in his narrative to study my face. He was scared of my reaction so finally I said, "Larry, I love you. Both of us fucked around before all this shit happened, so stop worrying. I'm not going to think ill of you." I grabbed him and kissed him to reassure him. He continued.

"Norm seemed to know when Monte would leave for New York. He showed up after work the first day that Monte went back to the city. I let him in and we made real wild love. Norm is an animal, without any finesse. He's inconsiderate of his partner, the exact opposite of you." He paused again and this time he kissed me gently with a closed mouth. A fire went through me.

"He left abruptly that first day. He had cum rather quickly but he had left me unsatisfied. He said that he had to get home to the wife and kiddies, the cheating bastard. After that he came around two or three times a week. I swear, Ken, I didn't want him to, but he wouldn't take no for an answer. If I objected, he said he would run me in on some imagined felony. That's how I found out he was a cop. Every time he made love to me, he hurt me. He liked fucking me without lube and worse, without a condom." Larry began to cry again and I held him tight. "The only time I got relief was when Monte was *in residence*. I wonder if he ever told Monte that he was fucking me. I sure never did."

"My poor baby," I said rocking Larry in my arms. "I swear I'll get that bastard, and if he's our man, I'll crucify him." Now I paused. I ran my hand up and down Larry's back to soothe him.

"Larry, baby," I said, "I want you to think hard. Can you think of any reason that Norman would want to kill all those guys?"

"Not really," he said, "but I could make some wild assumptions. Since they met, Monte has been showering Norm with gifts. Monte even gives him money to buy frivolous things for his wife and kids. When Norm goes into the city, he stays at Monte's plush apartment, and Monte takes him to every Broadway show running. But here's the big but! Monte found out what a great calligrapher Norm is, and he has him do the invitations for every one of his sex parties. We have at least one a month. Norm has been addressing the envelopes for several months now and not once has he been invited to a party. If I was Norm, I'd be pretty pissed at that myself. If I had to guess, I would think that Norm was afraid that Monte would tire of him and award the prize to one of his new play mates."

I didn't say anything to Larry, but I couldn't help thinking about the motive he was ascribing to Monte. **The same motive fit Larry to a tee.** I also remembered the looks that passed between Monte and Jason back at the house and I had to conclude that **Jason had the same motive**. I had a lot of suspects and no evidence.

Just then, Jason addressed me through the bars. "Hey Ken," he said. "Since we can't get hold of Norm, I asked the guys to ask his wife if she would please come by. I'd like to know if she can shed some light on his comings and goings this weekend. She should be here any minute. When we go to interview her, I've asked the guards to put Ian in your cell. You better look after him good, Larry. I've got a crush on him."

"You'd better take good care of Ken then," Larry hollered back. "I've got more than a crush on him." I heard Jason laughing. It wasn't long before one of the guards came and put Ian in my cell and Jason and I were taken to the interview room. I wondered why Jason was keeping Monte so isolated. Maybe it was some sort of revenge. But if it was revenge, what was it for?

Chrissy Sharpe looked agitated as we entered the interrogation room. "I don't have much time," she said. "I left the kids with my next door neighbor." She was a small woman, barely five feet tall and I doubted if she weighed a hundred pounds.

"I'll get right down to business then," Jason said. "When did Norm leave on this fishing trip?"

"Friday afternoon," she stated without hesitation. "He said he'd be gone the entire holiday weekend." The chief and I looked at each other. Norm was one of the officers who responded to his call Saturday morning. Well, we knew he lied to his wife about his sexual preferences, so it was natural that he would lie about his whereabouts. I wondered where he had spent Friday night. Perhaps lurking in Monte's hallways.

"Have you heard from him at all?" I asked. "We can't seem to reach him on his cell phone. She shook her head.

"He was going to some lake up in the Catskills. You know how bad reception can be in rural mountainous regions," she offered by way of explanation. She had read all about the murders, and it was obvious that she was beginning to look worried. Could her Norm have had anything to do with it? She concluded that it was impossible and she relaxed some.

Has Norm ever talked to you about Monte Barnes?" Jason asked.

"He's the guy who owns the house where those fags were murdered," she said. Jason's eyes became slits and I think mine did too. "No," she said, "I can't say as he ever has. How would he know any gays anyhow?"

Chrissy's belligerent behavior concerning gays was perfect evidence to me that she was lying. This beleaguered housewife knew all about her husband's escapades, or at least she suspected. Her facial expressions and uncharacteristic crude language were a dead giveaway. The lady was hurting inside.

"Is your husband in the habit of disappearing for extended periods of time without keeping in touch with you?" I asked her this in the kindest tone of voice I could muster up. If Monte was in the room, he would have immediately cast me in a play. As I asked that question I looked her straight in her eyes in the most compassionate way my acting abilities would allow. I could definitely see her softening.

"Yes," she answered. "He disappears often. I know he likes to go into the city a lot. He says he is going with friends, but I know he goes alone. The only thing that he is considerate about is that if I need it, he leaves me the car and takes the bus into Manhattan."

"I'm sorry to have to tell you this Chrissy," Jason said in a sad voice, taking a cue from me. "You said that Norm started his fishing trip Friday evening, but he was on duty Saturday. He got off about 3 PM and he's off until tomorrow morning. Do you have any idea where he spent Friday night?"

Chrissy lowered her head. "I should have known," she said. "If he didn't go into Manhattan then I have no clue where he was Friday night. He's cheating on me. Isn't he chief? I'd like to know who the bitch is."

"I have no idea," the chief lied.

"Is there anything else, Jason? I really need to get back to the kids."

Jason looked at me so I said to Chrissy, "That's it for now, but we might have to call on you again. In the meantime if you should hear from him, please ask him to call the precinct as soon as possible." Chrissy nodded and left.

Jason and I hurried back to our cells. We both were apprehensive about leaving Ian and Larry alone for even a second. When we got there moments later, we were both relieved to see that they were alive and well and playing a competitive game of "War." One of the guards must have given them a deck of cards. When they saw us, they stopped playing and were just as relieved to see us as we were to see them.

Before the guards reconfigured our cell arrangements, I looked in on Monte. "How are you doing fellow?" I asked him. He looked at me blankly. He seemed still to be in a state of shock.

"Okay, I guess," he muttered and that was that. Poor Monte. His whole world had turned upside down on him. Eight of his best friends and fuck buddies, had been murdered right under his nose, and at this moment in time his life sucked. He could be murdered himself at any time, or worse, he could be accused of murder. I tell you, I really felt for him. But my fears were all centered on Larry right now.

In the middle of the night, Larry and I were playing a game of sixty-nine when I heard a commotion in the next cell. Jason was yelling for the guard and using his cell phone.

"What's wrong?" I yelled.

"It's Ian, Jason sobbed. "He was down on me and he suddenly passed out. He's barely breathing. Oh God, don't let this be happening. Please don't let him die. I love him. I love him," Jason was getting hysterical and I couldn't blame him. If Larry was to pass out on me, I'd freak also.

Soon the paramedics arrived. They rushed into the cell and began to examine Ian. "I think he's in a diabetic coma," one of the EMT's said. "Does anyone know if he has diabetes? Search his pockets for insulin."

Jason went through Ian's shorts and found a bottle of insulin, but no needles. The paramedic took a syringe from his bag and administered a small dose of insulin to the comatose Ian.

"This will have to do until we get him to the hospital." The paramedics lifted Ian onto a gurney and started to wheel him away.

"I want to go with him," Jason yelled. "I'm afraid to leave him alone."

"That's not possible Chief," one of the guards said. I'll put a man on the case to watch over him until he's released from the hospital. Don't worry we'll take good care of him."

The ambulance blared its way to Nyack Hospital. The paramedics rushed Ian into the ER. A doctor quickly assessed the situation, drew some blood and did a shortcut test for blood sugar. Then he gave Ian a proper dose of insulin. The doctor drew a curtain around the gurney, and the jailhouse guard and the two paramedics accompanied the doctor to a desk where they filled out and signed all the necessary documents.

They had all failed to notice the dark figure that had entered the ER immediately after they all did. In spite of the hot and humid night, he was wearing a jacket with a hood. The hood was doing a good job of concealing his face. He ducked behind the curtain and was gone from the hospital long before the jailhouse guard returned. The guard positioned himself outside the curtain and kept a look out until two orderlies came to take Ian to a room.

The orderlies opened the curtain and gasped. Ian's face was covered with a pillow. They removed the pillow fearing the worst. The young man had been suffocated with the pillow, and had gone to join Monte's other guests wherever they were.

Chapter Six

One of the guards approached Jason's cell, unlocked it, and asked Jason to come with him. A moment later I heard Jason's blood curdling scream. Nobody had to tell me what had happened. I just knew. I wrapped Larry in my arms and this time I sobbed.

Two guards returned to the cell block and removed Monte, Larry and me from our cells. They took us to the interrogation room, where Jason was sitting at the table. His head and arms were on the table and he was crying. When we came into the room, he looked up. His eyes were red and swollen. In a very raspy voice he said, "The bastard got Ian too. He smothered him in the ER. I've issued an APB for the apprehension of Norman Sharpe. I don't know if he's the culprit, but I want him behind bars. In the meantime, I'm putting Monte in my cell right next to your cell. From now on whatever we do, wherever we go, it's going to be together. Not one of us is to be left alone, not for one second."

The guards took us back to our respective cells just in time for breakfast. Again we used the dog to test our meals. The K9 sampled food from all four trays before we dared eat anything. The four of us sat pretty quietly all day, not daring to speak. We were more fearful than any of us had ever been in our lives. Then late in the afternoon, Norman came running into the station house accompanied by two other guys. They all demanded to see the chief at once.

Jason had the guards put Larry and Monte in the same cell and took Jason and me to the interrogation room. When we got there, Jason gasped. Norman was standing there with two of Jason's top cops. They all had the same story. They were all off duty from early Saturday afternoon until Tuesday morning. Norm had left the station house on Saturday and gone home with Will. Sam had driven and he picked up Will and Norm. The three had driven directly to a secluded lake in The Catskills. Fishing had been good and Sam's van was loaded with fresh fish on ice.

On the way home after lunch today, Sam turned on his police radio and they heard about the APB which was out on Norm. They drove directly to the station house. Our chief suspect was in the clear.

"You'd better get that fish refrigerated," Jason said to Sam. "And take Will with you. Norm, you stay here. I have some more questions and I'll get you a ride home when we are through." The other two cops left and Jason asked the guards to leave him, Norm and me alone. When it was just the three of us, Jason closed the door. The three of us sat down at the table.

"Your wife said that you went fishing Friday, but you were on duty Saturday morning. Do you care to explain?"

Norm definitely looked uncomfortable. "I went into the city on Friday evening," he said, barely above a whisper. "I think you know why," he added.

"Did you get lucky?"

"Yeah!"

"Well you need an alibi for Friday night. I hope you have his name and number."

"I'm afraid not, Jason. He was someone anonymous I met in a back room. I swear, I took the last bus back at midnight and Will picked me up at the bus station and took me to his house. He can vouch for that."

Jason looked defeated. "Do you have any questions?" he asked, looking straight at me.

"Yes," I answered. "Norm where did you study calligraphy?"

"At the community college about two years ago. Why?"

"I'm asking the questions, please. Did anyone else you know take the class with you?"

"Yes, my wife, but I don't see what that has to do with the guys who were murdered in Mr. Barnes' house."

Norm referred to the murders in the house. Didn't he know about the others?

There was a pad and a pen on the table. I handed them to Norm and asked him to pen 201 River Street, just as he would if he were preparing an invitation for Monte. Norm reluctantly did as I requested.

When he was done, he asked if there were any more question. If not, he said that he really needed to get home and shower.

"One more," I said. "When your wife needs to leave your kids with a neighbor, who does she rely on?"

"Our next door neighbors, the Turners. We return the favor when they need a hand."

"Thanks," I said and nodded at the chief as if to say, *I'm done.*

Jason called a guard in and told him to get Norm home. Another guard came to take us back to our cells, but I requested another few private moments with Jason. When we were alone I recapped the situation with him as I saw it.

"Chief, Norm is totally unaware of any murders that have occurred since he helped remove the bodies from Monte's house. His alibi for Friday night is shaky, but Will did pick him up at the bus stop and he has been in the presence of policemen since Will picked him up, so unless your whole force are conspirators to murder, he's clean as a whistle."

"So where do we go from here?" Jason asked.

"I'd like to speak to Mrs. Turner or better still, if she knows who you are, I think you should speak to her."

"What do you want to know?" The chief looked confused.

"I want to know how often and when she had the Sharpe kids since Friday."

"There was a phone in the room. Jason used the intercom and asked whoever answered to get the phone number of the Turners who lived next door to Norm. In a minute or two, the phone rang and Jason wrote down a telephone number. He dialed and after two rings, Marge Turner answered the phone. The chief identified himself and asked her the questions that I had proposed. The chief turned white as he listened to Mrs. Turner's answers. He thanked her for her cooperation and hung up the phone.

"You'd better sit down," Jason advised me. "Marge Turner hasn't seen hide nor hair of the kids or Chrissy since Friday morning. She saw Chrissy load them in the car and drive away. She assumed that Chrissy had taken the kids to her parents' home in New Jersey for the long weekend. Marge said that as far as she knew, Chrissy never came back and the house is empty."

"Chief," I said, showing Jason the paper that Norm had written on. "This handwriting is totally different from the handwriting on my invitation. Norm did not address Monte's invitations to this party. Chrissy took the calligraphy class with Norm. When she was called in to the station, did your guard call her home phone or her cell phone? I assume you have both on file. The finger is pointing straighter and straighter at her."

A quick call confirmed that she had been reached on her cell phone.

"What would be her motive for multiple murders?" the chief asked.

"Hatred," I think. "She's homophobic and she found out about her husband's secret life. I think it was she who addressed the invitations. She assumed that Norm would be at the party and not at the fishing hole. She decided to eliminate us one at a time. She must have noticed that our first names were alphabetically consistent. By murdering one at a time in alphabetical order she was daring the police to play her game. I guess she figured Norm would be her last victim, and her revenge would be complete. Unfortunately, even though we guessed the sequence of murders, we were powerless to stop her."

The phone rang and Jason picked up. It was Norm reporting that his wife and kids were gone. Her closet was cleaned out, and most of the kids' clothing was gone also. He also said that on a hunch he went to his dresser drawer where he kept the key to Monte's house and it was not there.

I signaled Jason that I wanted to ask Norm a question.

"Hold on a sec, Norm. Ken wants to ask you something."

"Who addressed the envelopes for Monte's party?" I asked.

"I was too busy, so I gave the guest list to Chrissy and she did it this time. Monte is very generous. He pays us fifty dollars an invitation. Our tuition for the class was well spent."

"Thanks," I said. "Norm," I tried to make my voice sympathetic. "I don't think your wife is coming back. You'd better give us your in-law's address and telephone number. Your kids may be in danger. And get yourself back to the station. Do you have another car? If not take a cab."

"I'll have to grab a cab," he said. "I'll be right down." There was the sound of utter defeat in his voice.

The next couple of hours were hectic. Jason called the police in Englewood, NJ and filled them in on what we knew. We feared that Mrs. Sharpe would be going to her parents to get her kids and start running. Yes, he knew that was irrational, but she was suspect to a series of irrational murders. He gave them the address of her parents, and the plate number of the car she was driving. The Englewood police hurried to Chrissy's parents' home. She had picked the kids up and left their home more than two hours earlier.

State troopers apprehended her at the southern end of the New Jersey Turnpike and she was taken into custody. She confessed immediately to the crimes, but it was several days before she was extradited back to Nyack. In the meantime Norm went to get his kids and he arranged for a lawyer for his wife.

I called my precinct and told them that I was involved in a murder investigation, assisting the Nyack police and I needed another day to wrap things up. Monte, Jason, Larry and I were released and we all went back to Monte's house. Larry barbequed the steaks that he had removed from the deep freeze two days ago. It seemed like two years. After dinner, Monte asked me how in the world such a little woman could have managed so many heinous acts.

"I think that when she gave Larry the drug, she gave Abel a lethal amount. The autopsy will confirm that. When he was unconscious, she pulled him out of bed, and that's when he hit his head. When she was sure that he was dead, and his blood had stopped flowing, she cut off his cock and slit his throat. Thank goodness he was already dead. Then she dragged him out into the hall and tied him up with pillow sheets to Monte's door. The other murders were by ingested poison, poisoned pellets or knife wounds. We know she had the keys to Monte's house. It would have been easy for her to drive up after dark on Friday and park a few streets away. She was small and lithe and she could easily have remained hidden from all of us.

"The jail is always open and she could have found plenty of nooks and crannies to hide in there also. She must have known where the cell keys were kept so she had access to us while we were sleeping also. It was easy for her to administer poison in our food, to blow a dart at us or to enter a cell to stab a sleeping victim. I guess we'll have to wait for her confession to confirm all this. One thing is for sure. She planned this a long time and she planned it well. She must really hate Norm."

As I was speaking, Larry sat down beside me and rested his head on my shoulder. I put my arm around him and this set something in motion between Monte and Jason. Monte sat down beside Jason and kissed him full on his lips. "Thank you," he said to Jason, and Jason embraced Monte. All Jason's jealousy was gone, and their eyes met in fondness.

"Now guys, I don't know about you but I am really tired. I need a good hot shower and I'm off to bed."

Of course, Larry followed me upstairs. When we were alone, he said, "Please don't abandon me now that it's over. Let me go home with you. Besides being a great cook and housekeeper, I'm an actor and I think Monte owes you his life. That having been said, I think he'll finally give me a part in one of his plays, so I won't be freeloading off of you."

"Do you have any other talents?" I asked, mockingly.

"You know I do," Larry stated firmly. With that he pulled down my gym shorts and went to work. As my mind drifted higher and higher into paradise, I became aware that I would never be lonely or alone again. Larry's tongue caressed my body in such a pleasurable way, like nobody had ever pleasured me before. Was it because I loved Larry or was it because he was just that good a lover? I really didn't care. I abandoned myself to his love and to a life time of his companionship.

Epilogue

Larry moved in with me and changed my life. I had never realized what a void there was in my daily existence. His love revived my spirit and my will to live. Even when we didn't make love, we slept wrapped up in each other's arms. That made us feel like we were in some sort of cocoon, warm and safe. This was a new and very welcome experience to someone who was as much a loner as I was, and used to having slam bang, short period sex adventures.

Gone too, were my fast food dinners. I ate like a king now. Even when Monte gave Larry the lead in a new play he was casting, I always found dinner prepared for me when I got home. When Larry was acting I would still go to my favorite bar and socialize with friends, but I didn't go home with any of them. Instead I went to the theater to meet Larry after the show.

The mere sight of him sends shivers down my back. He has made me into a better, kinder human being. I now volunteer in the rehab of many of the individuals I have arrested. I help them reform and start new and productive lives.

I can't tell you how happy I am. Everyone should fall in love.

ABOUT THE AUTHOR

Hank Brooks was born in Brooklyn, NY and lived most of his adult life in and around the New York City area.

He is very active in SAGE, a senior advocacy group for gay men and women.

He has three children and five grandsons. He is a retired CPA, and now lives with his partner, Leo, in Coconut Creek, Florida.

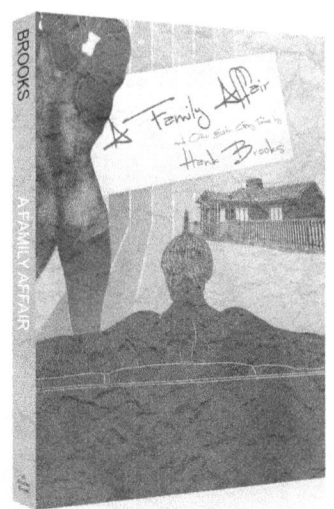

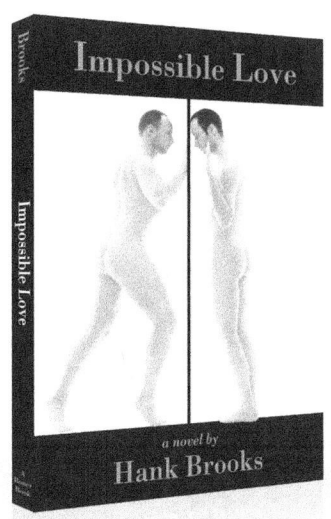

www.ingramcontent.com/pod-product-compliance
Lightning Source LLC
Chambersburg PA
CBHW051120260626

47170CB00005B/1597